CALEB'S WARS

by David L. Dudley

CLARION BOOKS

Houghton Mifflin Harcourt
New York | Boston | 2011

Clarion Books
215 Park Avenue South, New York, New York 10003

Clarion Books is an imprint of
Houghton Mifflin Harcourt Publishing Company.

www.hmhbooks.com

The text was set in Coldstyle.

LIBRARY OF CONGRESS CATALOGING-IN-PUBLICATION DATA
Dudley, David L.
Caleb's wars / by David L. Dudley.
p. cm.
Summary: Fifteen-year-old Caleb's commitment to justice and courage to protect
it grow as he faces a power struggle with his father, fights to keep both his
temper and self-respect in dealing with whites, and puzzles over the German
prisoners of war brought to his rural Georgia community during World War II.
ISBN 978-0-547-23997-2
[1. Conduct of life—Fiction. 2. Segregation—Fiction. 3. Family life—Georgia—
Fiction. 4. World War, 1939–1945—Fiction. 5. Prisoners of war—Fiction.
6. Germans—Georgia—Fiction. 7. Healers—Fiction. 8. Georgia—History—20th
century—Fiction.] I. Title.
PZ7.D86826Cal 2011
[Fic]—dc22
2011009644

Manufactured in the United States of America
QFF 10 9 8 7 6 5 4 3 2 1
4500313638

For Lucy Brown

with respect, admiration, and love

CHAPTER ONE

Wʜᴀᴛ's GOIN' ON down there—Klan meetin'?" Nathan pointed toward the corner of Main Street and Pine, just where we were headed.

Henry grabbed my arm. "It ain't really the Klan, is it, Caleb?"

Sure enough, the sidewalk ahead was jammed with folks—white folks. Even for a Saturday, it was a crowd. My stomach knotted.

"Course not," I told Henry. "It's just some white people, not the Klan."

"Same difference, ain't it?" Nathan asked.

"You're funny."

"I try."

"Time for us to get off the sidewalk," I said. "Look who's coming."

"The Hill boys." Nathan spat into the street.

"Only Lonnie and Orris," Henry said.

"Oh, well, we safe then," Nathan answered. "I reckon you can take two of 'em by yourself, big and brave as you is."

"Quit it," I told them. "We got to move now."

Henry looked at the street and shook his head. "Not me! That mud a foot deep. I ain't gonna wreck *my* shoes."

Lonnie and Orris, two of the three Hill brothers, nasty white trash who lived way back in the country, were coming up on us fast. We'd had a couple of run-ins with them before, and I didn't want to mess with them today.

"It's not that deep," I insisted. "Come on." I stepped down, and right away sticky red mud came up over my shoe tops.

"It ain't that deep," Nathan mocked.

"Outta my way, boy!" Lonnie Hill said. He and Orris were right in front of us. Lonnie shoved Henry, who lost his balance, fell off the sidewalk, and landed in the mud. Nathan jumped down, and the mud came over his shoes, too.

"Ain't they ever gonna learn?" Orris asked his brother.

"Not likely. Way too dumb," Lonnie said. They strolled away, laughing.

"Goddamn crackers," Nathan muttered. "Who they think they is?"

"White boys," I told him.

Henry pushed himself up from the mud. "I'm goin' home," he said. "Mama gonna get on to me about messin' up these new overalls."

"It wasn't your fault," I said.

"She didn't want me to come with y'all in the first place. Mama say you two always gettin' me in trouble."

"Stay home, then," Nathan told him. "We tired of draggin' you with us anyway. You ain't nothin' but a baby."

"And you ain't nothin' but a son of a bitch!"

Nathan pretended to be shocked. "Oooh! That any way for you to talk? And you gettin' baptized tomorrow."

"You, too. And how about the way you *act?* That way worse than the way I talk. 'Sides, it was you and Caleb taught me to cuss."

"You was a good student, though. Took to cussin' like a bull takes to a cow."

"Both y'all, quit," I told them. "Let's get to the post office and then go home."

"I ain't goin' to no post office," Henry declared. "Not with all this mess on me. I'm goin' home right now."

"It's on the way," I reminded him. "Just wipe it off. This bag is getting heavy, and I'm sick of toting it all over town."

"What'sa matter? Don't you like bein' your folks' errand boy?" Nathan asked.

"No, I don't. I'm sick of doing all Randall's chores and mine, too."

"You oughta remind your mama and daddy that slavery days is over," Nathan said. "Tell 'em you a free man."

"Oh, sure. And have Pop get all over me? No, thanks."

"If we goin' to the post office, come on," Henry said.

"Let's stay in the street, though," I said. "We can't get any muddier, and look at that crowd now." There were even more white folks standing on the sidewalk up ahead.

As we walked toward the corner, picking our way around pools of rusty red water, I realized what was going on. Davisville's new restaurant, the Dixie Belle Café, was opening today, and folks were waiting to go inside for dinner. By the door stood a girl wearing a fancy old-fashioned dress with a frilly full skirt. She held a little white umbrella in one hand and carried a basket on her other arm. People were reaching into it for slips of paper.

"She some pretty," Henry declared.

"She *white*," Nathan told him. "Don't you even *look* at her."

"Why not?"

Nathan swatted the bill of Henry's cap. "Ain't your daddy taught you nothin'? Black man look at a white woman the wrong way—*pow!* He *gone*."

"I know that! All I said was, she pretty."

"Yeah, she pretty, all right. Regular Scarlett O'Hara."

"Who that?"

Nathan often said Henry either was stupid as a guinea hen or had kept his head in the clouds so long, he didn't know a thing about the real world. Nathan was right.

"Just keep going," I told them. "And don't stare."

But Henry stopped in his muddy tracks. "Oh, Lord. That fried chicken sure do smell good."

"I swear," Nathan said. "You wanna live up to every one of them crackers' notions about us colored folks? 'Oh, Mammy, I jes' *got* to have me some mo' of dem collard greens and fried chicken. And don't forget de yams and de co'nbread!'"

I kept quiet. Nathan was funny, but if I laughed, it would only egg him on.

He kept it up anyway. "Lemme pull out my harmonica so Henry can do a little dance—entertain de white folks. Maybe somebody throw us a penny."

"Shut up!" Henry cried. "You got a big mouth."

A couple of white men glanced in our direction. We were talking too loud.

I glared at Nathan. "When are you gonna leave him alone?"

He shrugged. "When it ain't fun to mess with him no more?"

Just then, a man in the crowd said, "Well, if this ain't my day!" He held up his slip of paper and announced, "'Good for free fried chicken dinners for a family of four.'"

"Lucky dog," a man next to him said. "All I won was a free piece o' pie."

People laughed, and then someone opened the doors to the Dixie Belle from inside and the crowd moved forward.

We went around the corner and faced a mud hole as big as a pond stretching all the way across Pine Street.

"No way," Nathan declared. "Step in that and so long, brother!"

The sidewalk was empty on this side of the building, so I climbed back up and the others followed. We tried scraping the mud off our shoes, like that would help now. Mine were slimy with it, and I could feel water sloshing every time I took a step.

We passed the café, and Nathan and I were halfway up the block before I realized Henry wasn't with us. I hurried back to get him.

"What is it now?"

"Look in there."

On the other side of the café window stood tables covered in green and white checked cloths, with shiny chrome chairs around them. Directly by the window was a booth with seats covered in green leather. The table was set for dinner—silverware, napkins, and even a vase of flowers.

No wonder Henry had stopped. It looked as nice as something in a magazine.

Nathan came up behind us and the three of us stood gawking. Then a woman with menus led some people to the booth and frowned when she noticed us. We stayed put.

"Ain't no law against lookin'," Nathan said.

The woman gestured at us, shooing us to move along. Now I recognized her—Sondra Davis, who owned this place. Behind her, I could see customers waiting to be seated.

"Let's go, gentlemen," Nathan said. "Don't want to spoil they dinner. Havin' to think about niggers bound to ruin a cracker's appetite."

We set off again.

"I wouldn't eat in a place like that if you paid me," Henry declared.

"Ain't you the man," Nathan exclaimed. "Now that you thirteen, you all big and tough."

"I wouldn't!"

"Me neither. Can't stand to be in no room with all them sweaty white people. You know how funky they smell. Make me want to puke."

We all laughed at that.

"How 'bout you, Caleb?" Henry asked. "Would you eat there?"

"Hell, no!"

"Good thing we all agree, then," Nathan said, "'cause

none of *us* ever gonna be invited inside a place like that. Least not until Kingdom Come."

We walked on, but my mind stayed behind—at the polished window of the new restaurant, at the fancy tables, at the good smells of simmering greens and baking bread and frying chicken. I'd lied to Henry. I *would* eat there—any day.

If they'd let me.

Then I noticed a soggy piece of white paper on the sidewalk. I picked it up and read, "Good for one free slice of lemon pie, with the purchase of a meal. Welcome to the Dixie Belle Café!"

I wadded the paper into a ball and hurled it against a brick wall.

* * *

White folks were lined up inside the post office, so I took my place at the back, along with three other Negroes, to wait till the clerk had helped all her white customers. When it was finally my turn, I was given a letter from my brother and a cardboard tube addressed to Ma.

Nathan and Henry were waiting for me outside. We could hear what sounded like heavy trucks, so we went back to Main Street to see what was coming. Right away an army truck loaded with men passed by. Another followed, also full of soldiers—but not American soldiers. German prisoners of war.

Not only did the Dixie Belle open today—so did Camp Davis, a mile out of town. The government had built it to hold captured Germans brought here to help do farm work because so many of our guys were off fighting in Europe and the Pacific. Two hundred were supposed to arrive today, Pop had read in the paper. And here they were.

We stood on the sidewalk to watch, and other folks stopped to look, too. A third truck came along, and it stopped to let some people cross the street. I was able to get a good look at the men jammed into the back. Some had on denim jackets and pants. Others had taken off their jackets and showed long-sleeved blue shirts or white T-shirts. Still others had on pieces of their German uniforms. One man wore a long black coat, even on this warm day. Pinned on the front was a golden eagle holding a swastika in its claws. For a moment my eyes met his. Even from a distance, I could see they were pale blue. How many men have you killed? I wondered. Then the truck pulled away.

Beside us, a white man said, "Goddamn Huns. Why didn't they just shoot 'em all? Last thing we need around here is a pack of Nazis. Craziest thing I ever heard."

"Why it say 'PW' on they jackets?" Henry asked.

"'Prisoner of war,' dummy," Nathan replied.

There were eight trucks. After the last one had gone, we headed home. I was late, and Pop would be steamed. He'd run out of screws and had sent me to buy some; then

Ma had added flour, lard, and canned goods to my list. She made me promise not to lose her ration book, reminding me it was almost as valuable as cash money these days.

Maybe they wouldn't be mad when I told them I'd stopped to watch the prisoners arriving. Pop was kind of interested in all that stuff, now that Randall was in the army. But that probably wouldn't stop him from yelling at me. He always found some reason. And Ma would be fretting because her pies needed baking.

Tomorrow was going to be a big day at church. Henry and Nathan weren't the only ones getting baptized in Hale's Pond. I was, too.

CHAPTER TWO

IN FIFTEEN MINUTES we came to Toad Hop, just
north of Davisville, where we lived.

"So we goin' out this evenin'?" Nathan asked.

"That's the plan," I told him. "After midnight?"

"Count me in. What about you, big man?" he asked
Henry. "You comin'?"

"I dunno. It mighty risky."

Nathan rolled his eyes. "Here we go again. How often
you come with us by now—five times?"

"Six."

"And ain't you always had a good time?"

"Yeah."

"And has you ever come close to gettin' caught?"

"No. . . ."

"Then why you think tonight be different? 'Sides, I got a surprise for y'all."

Now Henry was interested. "Tell us."

"Only that I found where Daddy keep his moonshine. How y'all like to sample some this evenin'?"

"Sure," I said right away. "Where was it?"

"Buried in the corner of the shed. Big ol' crockery jar. Ain't no way to see the level in it, so Daddy never miss any."

"What about it?" I asked Henry. "You coming?" I was hoping he'd say no. He was scared of his own shadow, and that took the fun out of it. Nathan was different. From the first time I invited him, he was ready for anything, even stuff that would have landed us in big trouble if we got caught.

But that was one reason I liked it. Going out meant action, adventure—both hard to come by in a place like Toad Hop. Being colored upped the stakes and made our little outings even more exciting. I'd been going out at night for two years now, since I was thirteen and my brother Randall invited me. Mostly we'd just messed around—smoked when we could lay our hands on some cigarettes, swam in Hale's Pond in hot weather, helped ourselves to ripe fruit when the season was right.

Other times we settled scores with white folks who had

it coming. Like after Mr. George Prothero hit Uncle Johnny Taylor in the mouth because he claimed Uncle Johnny had sassed him. If Mr. George ever wondered who broke down a section of fence and let half his cows loose on the Augusta highway, he could have asked Randall and me about it. And like every other Negro in Toad Hop, we'd have told him, "We don't know nothin' 'bout dat, Mist' George, but we shore is sorry dat it done happen. Hope none o' yo' cows got hit."

Thinking of the old times made me miss my brother. The owners of the Dixie Belle Café needed a lesson in good manners. Randall wasn't around to help settle a score tonight, but if he were, he'd be all for it.

"Hey, Caleb, you all right?" Nathan's voice brought me back from my thoughts.

"Sure. I was just thinking about something else."

"Answer Caleb's question," Nathan told Henry. "You comin' with us or not?"

"I dunno. Drinkin's a sin."

"And smokin' ain't? That never stopped you," Nathan reminded him.

"Drinkin's different. Worse, Daddy say. And what about tomorrow?"

"What about it?"

"Gettin' baptized! Wouldn't be right to drink the night before we do it."

"Stay home, then."

"I don't want to."

"Then come on," I said. "Just make up your mind."

"All we gonna do is taste it," Nathan added. "Nobody gonna get drunk."

"I dunno."

"Look at it this way," Nathan began patiently. "Your daddy say baptism wash away our sins, right?"

"Yeah."

"So if drinkin' *is* a sin, then God gonna take care of it tomorrow mornin' when we go under the water."

"That's ignorant," I said.

"You got a better idea?"

"No—"

"Then shut up. You come if you want to," he told Henry. "Nobody gonna make you drink a drop, you don't want to."

"All right," Henry agreed. "I'm in."

"Okay. See you." He went on his way toward the church. Since his daddy was the preacher, they lived next door.

"There go one big baby," Nathan observed. "I hope he don't ever squeal on us. We be skinned alive if our daddies ever find out."

"We can keep Henry quiet."

"How?"

I had no idea. "Jeez, Nathan! Do I have to answer every one of your dumb questions? Besides, we won't ever have to shut him up."

"Why not?"

"'Cause we're not gonna get caught. That's what you told him."

"I hope you right."

"Trust me. I'll be under your window after twelve."

"Until then, my man."

He headed for home, and I thought that if Henry was a big baby, Nathan was a big pain in the ass.

* * *

Ma was waiting on the porch. "Where've you been?" she demanded. Then she noticed my shoes. "And what have you been doing—making mud pies?"

"Sorry, Ma. We had to walk in the street because there were lots of white folks on the sidewalks. The new café opened today."

"That still doesn't explain why you're late. If I don't get these crusts made, there won't *be* any of my pies at the dinner tomorrow. You eat in town?"

"No, ma'am." The booth in the Dixie Belle flashed in my mind.

"I kept something warm for you. Come in and I'll dish it up. But first take those screws to your father. He's already come looking for you three times."

"These came." I held up Randall's letter and the cardboard tube. Maybe Ma would forget she was annoyed with me.

"What a nice surprise! Hand me the bag and go get your father."

Pop was planing a board in his shop. As usual, his sleeves were rolled up, showing the thick muscles on his forearms. I was pretty big for my age, but Pop was a lot bigger—and a lot stronger. Only Randall had ever dared tangle with Pop, and Randall had always lost.

"'Bout time you home," Pop said without even looking up from his work. "Where the hell you been? Didn't I tell you I couldn't finish that cabinet without more screws?"

"We stayed to watch the prison trucks go by."

Pop put down his plane. "So they really here. Part of me didn't believe it could be true. But nobody best underestimate what that Lee Davis can make happen. What y'all see?"

So I explained, and then I told Pop to come on, Ma had a new letter from Randall. I ate warm beans and cornbread at the kitchen table while Ma read the precious letter.

"'Dear Pop, Ma, Caleb,

'I'm doing okay over here in Louisiana. Some of the boys from up north stay mad because of the way Negroes are treated down here, but I'm used to it.'"

"Hm," Pop snorted. "Word is, Louisiana worse than Georgia, and that sayin' a mouthful."

"'One fellow from New Jersey says we should demand better treatment, since the country is making us give our lives fighting the Germans and the Japs.'"

Ma put the letter in her lap. "I know Randall's right, but I pray he doesn't do anything foolish—get a reputation for complaining about things."

"It ain't him talkin'. Just sharin' what that guy from Jersey is sayin'. They treated our boys like shit in the last war, and you can bet nothin' changed. Negroes get drafted to go fight—and for what? I don't see no enemy armies invadin' Georgia. Why can't this country stay out o' other folks' messes? We got plenty problems need fixin' right here at home."

Now we were in for it. Pop would get going on his long list of what was wrong with the world, wrong with America, with Georgia, with Davisville, with white folks, with Negroes, and sooner or later, what was wrong with me. I didn't want to hear it. Especially not about the war. I was worn out with the war—tired and bored with all the bad news, tired of rationing food, tired of hearing about war bonds and President Roosevelt and Adolf Hitler.

"And how come Lee Davis boy ain't in uniform?" Pop grumbled. "Stewart Davis is every bit as fit as Randall, and he get a medical waiver! Looks like he gonna spend the war ridin' in that red roadster his daddy bought him while all the *poor* boys get theyselves killed."

"There must be a good reason," Ma replied.

"You right about that. Mr. Lee Davis *money* is the reason. He done *bought* his boy's ticket out of the service."

"We shouldn't judge when we don't know the facts."

"For God sake, Lucy! *Face* the facts."

"What else does Randall say?" I asked Ma. If we didn't distract Pop now, he'd never shut up.

"'Our training is going okay,'" Ma went on. "'I qualified as marksman yesterday. Pop, thanks for teaching me to shoot so good. The guys from the country are mostly all good shots because they been using guns all their lives. So I guess if I get into a battle, I will get me some Germans.'"

"He could get hisself some right here in Davisville," Pop noted.

Ma ignored that. "'The weather is hot and rainy, but I'm keeping my feet dry, like you told me, Ma. There is plenty of chow at every meal. I lost three dollars gambling Friday night, which is why my check ain't as much as we agreed on. Don't put any money in my account. It's all for you.'"

"Lost three dollars gambling!" Pop fumed. "That's three days' pay, case he forgot! I *told* that boy to watch out for card sharks and tricky dice men. Wouldn't surprise me if he was drinkin', too."

"Randall is a good boy," Ma said. "He's fighting to make the world a better place."

"Somebody oughta make *Davisville* a better place! I can't figure how havin' our boys die way over there is doin' one thing to help any Negro I know."

Ma closed her eyes for a moment, like she was tired.

"What else?" Pop asked.

"'The boys say we going to be sent overseas soon, but no one know for sure. If the officers know, they ain't talking. If we do get sent, I hope to have some leave first so I can see you. I hope you all are doing good there. Please keep writing. Your letters mean a lot to me. My love to everyone. Your son, Randall.'"

Ma gave Randall's check to Pop, then got up. "You two go on, and let me work in peace," she told us. "I have these pies to make."

Pop told me to come with him to his shop. "Your ma's right worried about your brother," he said as we walked in. "I don't know how she gonna handle it once he go overseas."

"He's really going?"

He looked at me like I was stupid. "Unless Roosevelt and Churchill can pull a miracle out of they asses and whup Hitler today! What you think Randall bein' trained for—a church social?"

Ma came into the shop. "I forgot to open my package. Look what it is." She held up a small banner a little larger than a piece of notebook paper. A red border went all around the edges; inside that was a white rectangle, and in the middle of that was a blue star. "I'm a Blue Star Mother."

"What that, Lucy?"

"An organization of mothers with boys in the service. The blue star stands for Randall. We can put this in a window to let everyone know we have a soldier in the family." Ma touched the banner reverently.

"I saw something like that in town," I said.

"That would be at the Durdens'," Ma replied. "Their boy Blaine got killed in the Pacific. If you lose a son in the war, you display a gold star banner."

"I can get it hung up," Pop said. "Lemme see it."

Ma handed him the banner and went back to the house.

"Blue Star Mothers," Pop mused. "Wonder if they know that Private Randall Brown is a Negro."

"What's it matter, Pop?"

"Plenty! How much you wanna bet that the Blue Stars is segregated, just like the United States Army?"

"The army's not segregated. Randall's in it, and lots of other colored guys."

"Negroes." Correcting me, as usual. "Ain't I already explained to you how it works? Sure, they let our boys in— to dig they ditches, tote they shit from one place to another, and do KP. Where the Negro officers? And the real combat training?"

There was no use arguing with Pop, but I couldn't help myself. "Randall wrote that he was getting to shoot."

"Big deal! The only weapon he probably ever gonna get to *use* in the United States Army is a potato peeler!"

"At least then he'd be safe."

"You want to smart-mouth me again, Caleb?"

"I wasn't smart-mouthing you."

"You want to talk back to me, then?"

There was no way to win against Pop. "No, sir."

"At least Randall had the guts to enlist before they come and got him," Pop said.

"I'd enlist if I was old enough." I didn't mean it, but it felt like the kind of thing Pop would want to hear.

"Hmph. Don't know that I see *you* in the service. They's more to bein' a soldier than goin' around raisin' hell."

That stung. "Want me to find a piece of dowel to hang that banner on?" I asked. I didn't give a damn now about Ma's Blue Star Mothers or what Pop thought about the army and Randall. The only thing I wanted was for Randall to stay safe.

CHAPTER THREE

AT MIDNIGHT I met Henry and Nathan, and we headed for the creek. It was as black as ink once we got into the woods. Henry tripped on something and fell down. Nathan laughed.

"I don't see nothin' funny," Henry grumbled from the ground.

"Where's your hand?" I asked.

"Here."

"Where?"

"Right here! Can't you see?"

"No, he can't see," Nathan said. "Ain't you noticed it dark out here?"

My eyes had adjusted now, and I yanked him up.

"It help if you skin was lighter," Nathan remarked. "But you blacker than a skunk."

"At least they ain't no white granddaddies in *my* family," Henry retorted.

"Both of you, quit. I'm sick of your mess."

"And I'm sick o' you acting like my boss," Nathan snapped. "You ain't in charge o' me."

"Somebody oughta be."

We felt our way to the fishing log. Nathan brought out the cigarettes and we lit up. Then he reached inside his shirt and brought out a pint bottle. "Here she is, boys. Who want to go first?"

"I guess I will," Henry volunteered. "Just a taste."

"You playin' with fire," Nathan warned. "You really gon' commit a big, bad sin the night before you get baptized?"

"Give it." Henry unscrewed the lid and took a sip. He made a face and then swallowed.

"How is it?" I asked.

"Okay. Burn, though. Here."

I took the bottle. Truth is, I'd never had a drink of moonshine before, and I felt nervous.

Henry was right. It felt like fire going down. "Not bad."

"Gimme," Nathan said. He drank a long swig, then passed the bottle back to Henry, who sipped a little more.

"How y'all like it?" Nathan asked. "Pretty sweet, ain't it?"

"It's all right," I lied.

"Have some more."

So we shared it around. It didn't take long for me to start getting lightheaded.

"How y'all feel about tomorrow?" Henry asked.

"Don't feel nothin' about it," Nathan said breezily.

"You better. We gonna be grown-up members of the church. Come tomorrow, we responsible for our sins."

"Let's go visit Rose right now, then," Nathan said. "Since we ain't responsible for nothin' we do tonight."

I'd heard that Rose would do it with anybody, but not for free. "You got the money?" I asked.

"Maybe."

"Nathan, you ain't never serious about nothin'," Henry said. "You really don't care about tomorrow?"

Nathan shrugged. "Hadn't thought about it."

"After everything Daddy taught us?"

"Don't know."

"Then why do it?" Henry asked.

"Mama want me to."

"What about your daddy?"

"He say they ain't no harm in it," said Nathan. "If I feel like doin' it, he fine with that."

"Don't you want it for yourself?"

"I reckon. Guess I need my sins washed away more than some folks do."

Henry didn't laugh. "What about you, Caleb?"

"Same as Nathan. I'm doing it for Ma."

"Your *daddy* sure don't care nothin' about it. My daddy say he ain't even a Christian. And you know what that mean."

"He goin' straight to hell, right?" Nathan said. "Lake o' unquenchable fire and all that mess. That what your daddy say?"

"Not exactly."

"Maybe you and your daddy should mind your own business," I said. "Let's go *do* something."

"Like head home and hit the bed," Henry declared. "I don't feel good."

"That 'cause you drunk, little man," Nathan told him.

"Am not!"

I could have sacked out, too, but there was a little thing to take care of first. "I have a plan. You boys up for a real adventure?"

"Sure." Nathan was ready.

"It's dangerous," I added.

"What?" Henry whispered.

"It's nothing for a boy," I told him. "It's man's work."

"What?" He sounded scared, like I hoped he would. Nathan was right: sometimes it *was* fun to mess with Henry.

"What say we go into town and pay the Dixie Belle a visit?"

"Now you talkin'," Nathan said.

"I ain't in this," Henry objected.

"Suit yourself."

"Come on," I said. "We'll take you home."

Henry protested, but not too much. We slipped through the shadows in Toad Hop, and Nathan gave Henry a boost up into his window.

Then Nathan and I went through the woods to Davisville and took every alley and deserted side street. At this hour, nobody was around.

Soon we were in the alley behind the Dixie Belle. I felt brave and powerful—ready to tear the building down brick by brick. I looked around to see what we could mess with. There were garbage cans, and a rat ran from us. Mops hung from pegs, brooms leaned against the wall, and some wooden crates sat in front of the door. Inside one were collards. Another was full of potatoes.

"I know," I whispered to Nathan.

"Steal 'em?"

"Nope. Something better."

I put the crates on the ground and pulled up their lids. Then I undid my fly and peed all over them. Nathan laughed and did the same. When we were done, we put down the lids and restacked the crates. Then we headed home.

I climbed in my window, got out of my clothes, and went to bed. Right away my head started to spin. Maybe I *was* drunk. Lying down was no good, so I propped myself against the wall. That's the last thing I remember.

* * *

Next morning I overslept, and Ma had to wake me. My head ached, and my stomach felt bad. But I couldn't let on.

I dressed and went into the kitchen. My place was set, but the rest of the table had been cleared. Ma was washing dishes.

"Where's Pop?"

"He got up early and took the wagon. Said he's going to cut wood this morning. You ready for something to eat? I got some grits, and I can fry you some eggs."

"Just coffee."

"Aren't you hungry?"

"No, ma'am."

"I guess you're nervous about your big day. How about a biscuit?"

"No, thanks. Pop's not coming to church?"

Ma put the coffee in front of me. "He never does. You know that."

"I just thought that maybe today . . ."

Ma sat down and reached her hand across the table. "You're disappointed. This day means a lot to you."

Truth be told, it didn't. Like I'd told my buddies, I was only doing it to please Ma—to try to make up for Randall's being gone, and for all the times I'd gotten into trouble.

"Yes, ma'am," I lied. "It does mean a lot."

Ma beamed. "You've made me so happy, son. Somehow I know in my spirit that this day is going to be the start of a new life for you."

"I wish Pop could believe that."

"You have to give him time. And . . ."

"And what?"

"Prove to him that you can change. No more fighting. No more stealing. No more talking back."

I'd heard this sermon before. "I'll do better, Ma. Starting today. I promise."

She went into the front room and came back with something wrapped in brown paper. "This is for you. Open it."

I undid the paper and found Grandpa Somerville's Bible inside. I was shocked. There wasn't anything Ma valued more than that Bible.

"I want you to have it. To mark the day of your baptism—the beginning of a new life."

"No, Ma. I know how much it means to you."

She put both hands on the tattered black cover. "Your grandpa read from this Bible every day of his life. He had it opened on his lap the morning we found him. He'd gone to heaven while reading from God's holy word."

I'd been hearing that little speech all my life, too. And now Ma would wipe away some tears, just like she always did.

Ma didn't disappoint me. "Your grandpa would have wanted you to have it," she assured me, dabbing her eyes with a handkerchief.

"Randall should have it. He's older."

She sighed. "Your brother's not walking with the Lord. He's chosen another path, the same path your father's walked all these years. But you, Caleb—I've always seen something in you: a heart for God, even these past couple years when you've fallen into temptation. I remember when you were young. You always insisted we ask the blessing at meals. And you never forgot your prayers before bed—"

"Ma, I—"

"You don't know how many hours I've spent on my knees, praying for you. And now that you're going to get baptized today, I know all my prayers have been answered."

What else could I do? I held on to the Bible. "I'll take good care of it."

"I know you will. But that's not the important thing. Promise me you'll *read* it."

I had to promise that, too.

Ma smiled, and for the first time in a long while, she actually looked happy. "Did I ever tell you that your grandpa blessed you when you were a little fellow?"

Plenty of times, I wanted to say. "I think you did. But I'd like to hear about it again."

So Ma told me the old, familiar story, how not long before Grandpa died, he asked to hold me. I wasn't very old, two maybe. They put me on his lap, and he laid his hand on my head and spoke a blessing, and said Father God had told him one day I would do great and mighty things for his kingdom.

What would Grandpa Somerville think of me now, if he knew that the night before I came to get baptized, I'd gotten drunk and then gone and pissed all over some white folks' food?

* * *

I looked for Nathan in the churchyard but didn't see him anywhere. Plenty of folks were around, though, all dressed up for the big day. I was wearing an old shirt and pants that would get soaked when I went into the pond, and Ma had bought me a new outfit for later.

Uncle Hiram and Aunt Lou saw me and headed my way. They weren't my real uncle and aunt, but I'd called them that ever since I could remember. All the young folks did.

Uncle Hiram was turned out in his best suit, complete with a starched, shining white shirt and string tie with a piece of turquoise set in the slide. He was right proud of that slide—said he bought it off a Navajo Indian chief way over in New Mexico a long time ago. Pop said Uncle Hiram just liked to tell stories—the old man had never been out of the county, let alone Georgia.

"How you, Caleb?" he asked. His big smile showed that half his teeth were gone. "Big day, ain't it?" He put out his hand, the knuckles all swollen and fingers twisted and curving toward his little finger. Rheumatism, Uncle Hiram called it. When I was little, his hands scared me, made me not want him to touch me. Now that I was older and understood, I felt sorry for him. Rheumatism was no joke. It made his hands hurt bad and twisted them up, but that never stopped him. Old as he was, Uncle Hiram could still do a hard day's work. Like he reminded everyone, there wasn't any choice—not if he wanted to eat.

I shook hands but didn't squeeze tight, the way Pop had taught me to shake. I wouldn't hurt Uncle Hiram for anything. He'd always been good to our family. He was praying for Randall every day, and that had to count for a lot, as good a man as he was.

The skin of his palm felt tough against my hand, and I could feel where it was hard with calluses. He could hardly close his fingers enough to give a real shake, but I didn't mind. He was doing the best he could.

"I been prayin' for you, Caleb," Uncle Hiram told me. His pale eyes were gentle. "Askin' Father to enlighten yo' mind and lead yuh in paths o' righteousness for his name sake."

"You makin' yo' mama right proud this day," Aunt Lou added. She was a tiny woman, especially compared to Uncle Hiram, who was tall and thin—a beanpole, Ma would have said. Aunt Lou had on a long, dark skirt, all the way to her shoes, a long-sleeved blouse with a brooch pinned at the neck, and a knit shawl over her shoulders, even on this warm spring day.

"Y'all hear from Randall lately?" she asked.

I started to tell them we'd had a letter yesterday, but Brother Johnson appeared at the church door and spotted me. "Come on inside," he called to me. "It's gettin' late, and you ain't even in your robe yet."

"Run on, now," Aunt Lou told me, reaching up and patting my shoulder. "I'll get Lucy to tell me about Randall during the picnic."

"God bless you, son," Uncle Hiram added. "I got the feelin' this is gon' be a big day in yo' life."

I didn't know about that, but I thanked them and let Aunt Lou kiss my cheek.

Inside, people were taking their places on the wooden benches. Everyone was talking. There always was a big crowd on baptism days—Pop said nobody in Toad Hop would ever miss the free dinner that followed the service.

"Here," Brother Johnson said, handing me a white choir robe. "Y'all sit up front, 'cause I got some special words for you in the sermon. At the pond, do just like we practiced."

"And keep our mouths and eyes closed," Henry added helpfully.

"That's right," Brother Johnson said. "I put my hand over y'all's noses. Y'all be okay. It only take a second. Now go to the back and get your robes on. And remember, boys: listen real careful to the sermon. The Lord got somethin' important to say to you today. God bless you."

We went to the back. Ma appeared, smoothed down the shoulders of my robe, and turned me around so she could make sure my shirt collar wasn't sticking up.

"I'm so proud of you," she told me. "Today you're a man in the eyes of God. If only . . ."

I guessed what she was thinking. Pop and Randall.

"Never forget this day," she said.

That morning went by in a blur. I remember sitting on the front bench along with Nathan and Henry, and how we were the only ones up there. I remember feeling lots of eyes looking at the back of my head. I remember Brother Johnson preaching a long time, but what he talked about, I don't know. My mind went everywhere except his words—to drinking the moonshine with Nathan and Henry, to the fancy table on the other side of the window at the Dixie Belle Café . . .

At last the service was over. My shirt was soaked, and I wanted a glass of water real bad. Someone started a song, folks began to clap, and Brother Johnson led us to Hale's

Pond—a two-minute walk. Behind us, people were shouting "Hallelujah!" and "Praise Jesus!"

On one side of me, Henry was clapping and shouting, too. He looked happy, the way the old folks did when the Spirit fell and they got joyful in the Lord. I'd never seen Henry look that way before.

Nathan was trying hard to keep from laughing. He rolled his eyes when I glanced at him. Maybe he was wishing this whole thing would be over soon and he could take off that silly white robe. That's just how I felt.

Folks gathered at the pond. The music continued. "Down by the Riverside," then "What a Friend We Have in Jesus." It felt like the singing went on forever. More than anything I wanted a big drink of water.

At last, Brother Johnson called for quiet. He prayed again. My stomach growled. Then he waded into the pond up to his waist, and Henry went in after him. Brother Johnson put one hand on Henry's back, the other over Henry's nose, and cried, "Henry Jefferson Johnson, I baptize you in the name of the Father, and of the Son, and of the Holy Ghost." He pushed Henry backward under the water.

Henry came back up, raised both hands over his head, and shouted, "Oh, hallelujah! I'm saved! Thank you, Lord!" He was grinning from ear to ear.

"Sweet Jesus," Nathan muttered. I knew better than to look at him.

Henry came out of the pond, his robe clinging to him. His mama met him with a towel, and he let her take him into her arms. "I'm saved, Mama!"

Then it was Nathan's turn. He went into the water and stood in front of Brother Johnson like an innocent little lamb. I had to bite my lip.

"Nathan Rodney Washington, I baptize you in the name of the Father, and of the Son, and of the Holy Ghost," Brother Johnson declared, and then he dunked him under. It seemed like he held Nathan down a good long moment. Anyway, he came out of the water sputtering and some folks in the crowd laughed, but not in a mean way.

"Bear fruit that benefits repentance," Brother Johnson said to him. "Welcome to the family of faith."

"Yes, sir," Nathan said in his most polite voice.

"Are you saved, son?" someone in the crowd shouted.

"I sure do hope so. Mama say if I ain't, she gon' make me do this till I am!" Everyone laughed.

"Caleb?" Brother Johnson asked. "You ready?"

"Yes, sir."

"Come on, then, and get your sins washed away."

The bottom of the pond felt squishy under my bare feet, and the water was cool on my legs.

"Caleb Thomas Brown, I baptize you in the name of the Father, and of the Son, and of the Holy Ghost." Brother Johnson put his hand over my nose, and I closed my eyes and mouth. Then I was pushed backward under the water.

For some reason, I opened my eyes. Everything was green and murky.

A strong, deep voice called, "Caleb!"

Then I felt myself being lifted from the water.

A voice said, "Behold my servant." The words were pretty loud, just not real clear.

"I beg your pardon, Brother Johnson. What'd you say?" I wiped the water out of my eyes and waited for him to repeat his blessing.

He looked at me, puzzled.

"What did you say to me?"

"Nothin'."

"Yes, you did. You called my name while I was underwater and said something else as I came up."

"I didn't say nothin', Caleb. You mistaken."

I wanted to tell him not to joke with me, but I could see he wasn't.

"Be faithful unto death, and I will give you a crown of life," Brother Johnson pronounced over me. "Welcome to the family, son."

I came out of the water, and there was Ma. She gave me a towel and helped me get out of my robe. I wanted to say something to her, ask her something—but what?

I sat on the grass and pulled my shoes on.

"Run on home and change," Ma told me. "We'll see you in a minute."

I started to go.

"Caleb?"

"Ma'am?"

"You are saved, aren't you?"

I wasn't sure if I was or wasn't. I had to figure out where that voice had come from.

"Yes, ma'am. I am."

"You've made me so happy!"

At home, I took off my wet clothes and began to dry myself. I was standing beside my bed when a voice said, "Behold my servant"—the same thing I heard when I was under the water.

I put the towel over my privates. Who was looking at me without a stitch on?

"Very funny, Nathan," I said. "You can come out from under the bed. You got me, all right? Joke's over."

Nothing.

I looked under the bed. He wasn't there. Then I looked out the window. Not there, either.

I wrapped the towel around myself and looked in the hall, the sitting room, and the kitchen. Even my folks' bedroom. There was no one in the house but me.

Back in my room, I sat on my bed, feeling all shaky. "Who is it?" I asked out loud. "What's going on?"

"Behold my servant," the voice said for the third time. This time I didn't hear it with my ears. It came from inside me, from deep in my belly.

"Stop!" I cried. "Stop it!"

It did. Everything was quiet. Suddenly I wanted air. I took a long, deep breath and held it. Then I listened to the sound of it coming back out—slow and soft.

I was still sitting on the bed, naked, when someone knocked on my door.

"Caleb? It's Ma. You in there?"

"Yes, ma'am. Let me finish putting on my clothes."

"Brother Johnson already asked the blessing. Come on while there's still something left."

"I will. Don't wait for me."

The sound of her steps faded, and then the back door closed.

I put on my new pants and shirt. In the hall, my face in the mirror looked just like always: dark brown skin, brown eyes, flat nose, and black hair cut short against my head.

But something new was going on inside me. Something I didn't understand.

CHAPTER FOUR

ALL THE WOMEN in the church cooed over me during dinner. All the men shook my hand. People paid me a lot of compliments, too, like how I'd grown up to be such a fine young man, and no wonder Ma was so proud of me. They reckoned I'd be a credit to the colored race, and who could say how Jesus would use me, now that I was saved and a responsible adult member of his church. I let myself be kissed by old ladies with whiskery chins and nodded and said thank you to all the usual polite things folks told me. I ate, but the food didn't taste good, not even Ma's blackberry pie. I *had* to talk to Nathan and make him tell me how he'd tricked me. How'd he get into the little attic where Ma kept boxes of Randall's and my baby clothes? That had to be it. He got up there and put his mouth down on the attic floor to mess with me.

But when I accused him, Nathan looked at me funny and I had to pretend I'd made the whole thing up. That made me feel like a fool.

* * *

Later that afternoon Pop said he was worn out from cutting wood and went to nap in his room. Ma went visiting. I went over to Nathan's place, but his mama told me he'd gone fishing with his daddy.

Back home, I napped, too, and dreamed strange things. When I woke up, I sat on the porch and tried to make sense of it all. A voice *had* called my name; then it spoke to me when I came up from the water and twice in my room. It sounded like a Bible verse, but I wasn't sure. And voices don't come out of nowhere. I'd just imagined everything— or dreamed it. In my bedroom I'd fallen asleep for a moment and dreamed someone was speaking to me.

You fell asleep *standing up naked?* I thought. Sure you did. And mules can fly.

There was one other explanation—the one I'd been trying not to think about. As crazy as it sounded, it might be true: *God* had called me by name, and then said, "Behold my servant." I wanted to tell Ma about it—I would, when she got home. And then she'd make me tell Pop, and we'd all talk about it. Maybe that would help change his mind about God and religion. And me.

Like a fast answer to prayer, Pop came through the front door. There was no reason to wait for Ma. I could tell him right now. But Pop's face told me he was in one of his moods. All my brave ideas disappeared faster than drops of water on a hot skillet.

"Hey, Pop. I was just going to feed the chickens." I started to get up, but he pushed me back.

"You got time. Your ma say I owe you a explanation."

"About what?"

"Why I can't stand religion or anythin' to do with it."

Pop had been telling me all his reasons my whole life. "You don't owe me anything."

"That how *I* feel, but your ma ain't gonna be satisfied until she get her way."

Pop was the one who always got his way, not Ma.

"You know I was raised up in church," Pop began, "and by the time I was your age, I had it all figured out. It's all part of the white man plan to keep us down. Preacher never talked about nothin' except 'bearin' our burdens with patience' and 'the trials of this world can't hold a candle to the glories of heaven.' It warn't nothin' but propaganda, and it's the same thing today. Then I got drafted into the army and saw how we was treated. And the Negro chaplains took the same old line."

Please don't let Pop get going on *that*, I thought.

"But I told you about that before, right?"

"Yes, sir."

"Then, after the war was over and I come home, my brother got killed."

"In the sugar mill accident," I recalled. This was another of Pop's favorite stories.

"Because the rich white men what owned the mill didn't care two cent about the safety of they workers. Then they was that explosion—"

I knew the rest. It had been so bad that they never found anything of my uncle Ronnie to bury.

"And of course they warn't no insurance to help his wife and kids. Owners give Esther fifty dollars—like *that* could help! But that warn't the worst. We was at home, receivin' visitors. There warn't no coffin—no need for one. I think that hurt Esther most of all. She didn't even have Ronnie's dead body to grieve over, and the kids couldn't understand where they daddy had gone. How do you explain to a child that one minute a man is there—big, strong man like Ronnie—and the next second he ain't nothing but a mess on the floor?"

Pop looked sad, and I felt sorry for him. I knew how bad I'd feel if it were Randall.

"Worst part was when the preacher come by the house. He sat down next to Esther and told her it was all part o' God's plan, and since God needed Ronnie to be with him in heaven, we had to accept his will and let him go. I never heard such a load of shit in my life! And Esther sittin' there, takin' it all in like it was gospel truth! Made me so sick, I had to leave the room. That was the last straw."

I could see Pop's point, but the preacher had only been trying to help. Was it his fault if Pop took it the wrong way? Suddenly I wanted to defend myself for getting baptized. "I only did it for Ma!"

"I know it. That the only reason I *let* you do it. Give her a little comfort when she need it so bad. When it come to religion, she a typical woman: don't want to ask no hard questions, just want it to help her feel good. I ain't interested in tearin' down her faith. They might not be too much harm in you joinin' the church to please her, long as you keep you head on straight and don't let nobody do your thinkin' for you. Promise me that."

"I promise."

"Now you can go feed the chickens."

CHAPTER FIVE

WHEN MA CAME HOME from her visiting, I
was ready to tell her everything, but there was no chance.
She had a headache, and Pop wanted his supper, and after
the meal was served and cleaned up, Ma went on to bed.

Sleep wouldn't come that night, and I got worn out
turning one way and another. Finally I pulled on my clothes
and slipped out the window. But when I got to Nathan's, I
didn't feel like waking him. I went over to Hale's Pond and
sat at the end of the dock. The baptizing place was nearby—
where it had all started. Uncle Hiram had said it would be
a big day for me, but this was more than I had figured on.

I could allow that God had spoken to me. But there
was a question I couldn't answer: Why?

I was only . . .

To all the white people I knew, I was just another nigger, and what use were nigger boys to God?

A colored boy? No, a *Negro* boy, the respectable term for people like us. Or was I more grown up now? The folks at church had called me "a fine young man." But I felt more like a punk kid who'd drunk too much whiskey the night before his baptism and peed it out on perfectly good food just to get even with some white folks. Like *that* would make any difference to the world.

So what could God want with someone like me?

"Nothing," a cruel voice inside me said. "Not one thing."

"Behold my servant." What was that about? Plenty of colored folks—Negroes—were servants, like the women who cooked, cleaned house, and did laundry for white ladies. Like the men who did yard work and answered the door in rich folks' houses. First we were slaves, then we were servants, and from what I could tell, we'd never had a choice. I didn't want to be anybody's servant, especially not a white person's.

"What do you want from me?" I asked God.

Above me, the sky was black, with lots of stars.

"What do you *want?*"

I lay down and looked up into that darkness, hoping for an answer.

The next thing I knew, it was dawn, and I had to run

home before the folks missed me. There had been no dreams, no voice—nothing.

As I got undressed, I thought again about telling Ma what had happened. Then I decided not to. Not when I felt so confused. But if I asked God again . . .

I got on my knees by my bed, bowed my head, and prayed.

For an answer there was only the ticking of the clock in our sitting room.

* * *

Next afternoon, when my chores were done, Ma told me I could go hang around with Nathan and Henry. It had been a long day with nothing much to do. School would have kept my mind busy—studying my books or, more likely, the pretty girls in my classroom—but school had been done for a few weeks already. At least for colored kids, it had. We had a short school year so we could help with plowing in the spring and with harvesting tobacco, peanuts, and cotton in the fall.

I found Nathan and Henry chopping wood for Miss Annie Ruth, a widow lady with no one to help her do hard work. She paid them what little she could, although Henry liked to brag that he'd do it for free, seeing how it was an act of Christian charity. I watched until they finished, and then we went off, Henry and Nathan each with a dime in his pocket. Henry suggested we go to town and buy some

Cokes, but Nathan didn't want to go that far. Instead, he suggested we visit the prison camp and see what was going on. We started down Brinson's Mill Road.

I wanted to tell my friends that God had spoken to me. Henry would be impressed—that much I knew. But Nathan, he'd think I was crazy and would say so, too.

As we walked, I found myself listening, waiting, in case God spoke to me again.

"What you so quiet about?" Nathan asked me. "You ain't sayin' nothin'."

"I don't have anything to say. Not everybody has to run their mouth all the time."

"You mean like I do?"

"You're the one who said it."

"What y'all think about yesterday?" Henry asked.

"Food was mighty good," Nathan said. "I had the belly-ache last night. Too much pie."

"That ain't what I mean. What about gettin' baptized?"

Here was my chance. I could come right out with it, casual-like, and see how they reacted.

Nathan didn't give me that chance, though. "I thought your daddy was gonna drown me. Seem like he held me under a long time."

"That's 'cause you had so many sins to wash away," I reminded him.

"Ha ha. What about *you?*"

This was my invitation. But I didn't take it after all. "I was all right. Didn't even get any water up my nose."

"But how did y'all *feel?*" Henry wanted to know. "In you souls."

"My *soul* was feelin' all right," Nathan said. "It was my *lungs* that wasn't feelin' too good."

"Be serious! I mean, did y'all get saved? *I* did."

"I guess so," Nathan answered.

"Praise the Lord! You repented of your sins?"

Nathan shrugged. "I reckon. What sins you got in mind?"

"All of 'em! I repented for smoking. I ain't never gonna smoke again. I promised the Lord last night I wouldn't."

"What else?" Nathan asked. He was trying not to laugh in Henry's face, but Henry didn't notice.

"I promised God I wouldn't cuss no more, or tell lies, or steal nothin', or . . . think about girls in a lustful way."

"Sounds like you fixin' to be a real saint," Nathan said. "What you gonna do for fun from now on?"

"Leave him alone," I said. "He's trying to be serious."

"That's right," Henry agreed. "From now on, I gonna live my life for Jesus, do what he say, and try hard not to do what he don't like."

"What made you decide all that?" I asked.

"The Lord spoke to me after I come up out of the water, told me I needed to start livin' a holy life, 'cause I gonna be a preacher!"

That got my attention. God had spoken to Henry, too?

"Hey, what is it?" Henry asked me. "You look funny, Caleb."

"Nothing," I lied. "I'm surprised you're gonna to be a preacher, that's all. You really hear God?"

"Naw. Daddy told me that stuff only happen in Bible days. The Lord don't talk to people in this day and time."

I wanted to tell him that his daddy was dead wrong. But then he'd go and snitch, and Brother Johnson would want to ask me a lot of questions and prove from the Bible how *I* was wrong . . . Suddenly, it just didn't seem worth all the mess.

"It warn't a voice I could hear," Henry said. "It was more like—like knowin' inside o' me."

"That ain't no surprise," Nathan pointed out. "Your daddy a preacher, you gonna be a preacher."

"That ain't it! You gonna be a bum just 'cause your daddy one?"

Nathan went for Henry then, and I had to pull him off. Truth is, his daddy, Mr. Artie, *was* a bum, and Nathan was touchy about it.

"We'll see just how long your 'decision' about holy livin' lasts," Nathan told Henry. "Won't we, big man? No more cigarettes, no more of my daddy's moonshine, no more cussin', no more—"

"God'll help me! And he help you, too, when you really ready to repent. *You* ain't been saved."

"Guess I jus' gotta take my chances, then. If gettin' saved make people act like *you,* I can do without it."

"How 'bout you, Caleb?" Henry asked. "You really get saved yesterday?"

At that moment I was so sick of Henry that I felt like punching him, too. "If I tell you, will you shut up about it?"

"All right."

"I don't know. I don't feel any different. Maybe I did and just don't realize it yet. And that's all I'm gonna say." If only Henry knew how much more I *could* say . . .

The camp was nothing fancy, just wooden buildings with metal roofs. It reminded me of Fort Gordon up in Augusta, where we'd gone when Randall got inducted into the army. All around this camp, though, were two wire fences a few feet apart—an inner and an outer one—each topped with three strings of barbed wire. At the corners were guard towers, and in them were men holding rifles.

A soldier appeared from the guardhouse at the gate. He had a rifle, too. "What do you boys want? This is no place for you to be hanging around."

"We ain't doin' nothin'," Nathan said.

"There's nothing to see here," the guard persisted. "You fellas better move along."

He was annoying me. "No harm in us looking, is there?" I asked.

"Get moving." It sounded like an order.

"Let's go," Henry whispered. "We don't want to get in no trouble."

"How we gonna get in trouble standin' in a public road?" Nathan shot back.

I had an idea. "Come on. Follow me."

"Bye," Nathan said cheerily to the guard. He ignored us.

I led the way back a little farther along the road and cut into the woods.

"What we doin'?" Henry asked.

"Going back to the camp. No one can tell us we can't stand and look. We weren't doing anything wrong."

"I ain't goin' back there."

"Fine," Nathan replied. "Run on home to your mama. She got your baby bottle all ready."

"We're just gonna look at the camp where there aren't any guards," I explained. "Nothing can happen."

"I don't know—"

"Do it say in the Bible, 'Thou shalt not look at the camp'?" Nathan asked.

Henry laughed. "I reckon not. I'm with y'all."

We came back to the camp halfway along its left side as you faced it from the road. The corner guard towers were pretty far away, and no one was watching the fence. We walked right up to it and looked inside.

Two prisoners were stringing a clothesline from the corner of a barracks to a pine tree. Others were digging a ditch. From a shower house came three men with wet hair, towels draped over their shoulders.

We walked toward the far corner of the camp and ducked into the woods to avoid the guard tower. Then we came around to the back, where a large space had been cleared and several prisoners were playing soccer.

A couple of men watching the game noticed us. "Hallo!" one shouted.

"What now?" Henry asked.

"Say hey back," I said.

"We won't get in trouble?"

"You can't get in no trouble sayin' hey to somebody," Nathan said.

The prisoner who'd said hallo started talking to the others. Then the soccer stopped, and in a moment, several of the men were looking at us and talking to each other.

"Come on," Henry said.

"Yeah," Nathan agreed. "They lookin' at us like we monkeys, even if *they* the ones in the cage."

As we went, I heard, real clear in the middle of all the German I didn't understand, one word I knew: "niggers."

Nathan and Henry heard it, too.

The soccer players started back to their game.

"Let's get out of here," Henry said.

"Wait," I said, searching for a rock. Nathan did the same. In a moment, I had three.

"What you gonna do, Caleb?" Henry asked.

I ran to the fence and let fly. "Hey!" I shouted.

"Go kiss Hitler's ass!" Nathan yelled. "But mine first!" Quick as anything, he dropped his pants and flashed his behind at the camp.

I threw another rock, and by a miracle it went through both fences and hit a prisoner in the head. Some others started for the fence, yelling.

"*Now* it's time to go!" I cried. "Come on."

Nathan gave the men his middle finger. I did the same. Some of the Germans returned the favor, so they knew exactly what we meant. Then, laughing, I ran back to the woods, Nathan and Henry right behind me.

"We showed 'em!" Nathan crowed when we stopped for breath. "That was a mighty lucky shot."

"You did your part!"

"I meant it, too. Any time they want to line up, I'm ready."

"Y'all shouldn't of done that," Henry protested.

"Why not?" Nathan cried. "They insulted us."

"We suppose to turn the other cheek."

"I *did!* Both of 'em! Jeez, I was obeyin' God without even knowin' it!"

"You better not take the Lord's name in vain."

Nathan turned on him. "Listen. If you want to get all holy, okay. I can put up with you bein' a pain in the ass for a while. But don't go tellin' *me* how to be, understand?"

Henry lowered his eyes. "All right. It just that I'm worried about you."

"About my soul, I reckon," Nathan said wearily.

"Yeah."

"Look. I can take care o' myself. Caleb, too. So just relax, okay?"

"All right."

We went through the woods, Nathan and me joking about how we'd insulted the Germans. Then, after we came back to Brinson's Mill Road, I heard the wagon. The sound came up behind us pretty quick, like the driver was in a hurry. "Move," I told Nathan, touching his shoulder. I didn't want to get run over.

When I turned to see who it was, something hit me right in the face—hit me hard. I touched my mouth and found blood.

"What the hell?" Nathan cried.

The wagon pulled up beside us. It was the Hills: Lonnie and Orris, the ones we'd met in town on Saturday, and their big brother, Dolan. They were laughing like the jackasses they were.

"You got him good." Lonnie gave Dolan a congratulatory slap. "Right in his big black mouth."

"Why'd you do that?" I cried. "We weren't bothering you."

"Look," Nathan said, picking up something from the road—a purple and white turnip. "This is what got you."

Without warning, another one caught Henry in the forehead.

"If this ain't my day!" Dolan crowed. "Got him, too! Jes' one to go."

"Come on," Henry urged. "They drunk."

Sure enough, there was a whiskey jug on the seat.

I didn't want to tangle with the Hills, especially not all three at once. They were mean enough when they were sober, and Dolan was a big guy.

"Don't turn your backs on me!" Lonnie shouted at us. "Look at me when I'm talkin' to you."

We all turned around. A lifetime of training made us do whatever any white man told us—even a sorry cracker like Lonnie Hill.

"So talk," Nathan said. "I can't wait to hear what somebody brilliant as you got to say."

"Hush!" I hissed at him.

"You got a smart mouth, you know that?" Lonnie said. "One thing I hate, it's a nigger with a smart mouth."

"You know what *I* hate?" Nathan asked.

"Don't!" Henry begged. He looked scared out of his wits.

"What'd that be?" Lonnie asked.

"That a woman old and ugly as yo' mama charge half a dollar. The boys in Toad Hop say she ain't worth more'n two bits."

In a second they swarmed off the wagon and charged us. Now we had to fight, and we did.

It's a good thing the Hills had been drinking—else they might have whipped us bad. They were fit to be tied, and Henry wasn't much help at first. I thought he was just going to stand there and "turn the other cheek" after Orris punched him in the face, but he got mad and fought back as best he could. Nathan took Dolan out with a quick knee to the crotch. Then we fought Orris and Lonnie. I got in my licks against them both, and so did Nathan, who could scrap like a cornered bobcat when he was really angry.

When it was over, we hightailed into the woods, leaving Dolan on the ground clutching his nuts, Orris with a nose pouring blood, and Lonnie with a gash on his cheek. Henry's face was a bruised mess, Nathan had lost part of a front tooth, and I had a split lower lip and a right eye swelling shut.

"I could choke you," I told Nathan when we were safely away from the road. "That cracker is right. You *do* have a smart mouth."

"Why you mad at *me?* Maybe you don't care what white folks say, but I'm sick and tired of bein' called a nigger. I'm gonna fight back every time trash like them boys mess with me."

"And get yourself killed," I predicted.

"Y'all both shut up!" Henry shouted. "Just shut *up*. We in bad trouble now, and y'all can't do nothin' but fight each other. What gonna happen when them boys get home and tell they daddy?"

"Nothin'," Nathan said. "They old man sorrier'n they is. Long as they bring him his liquor, he won't care if they get they white asses killed."

Henry wiped away tears. I wanted to smack him.

"Nathan's right," I said. "Nothing else will happen."

"You don't know that! It's all your fault," Henry accused. "You, too, Caleb. If y'all hadn't of throwed them rocks at the prisoners, them boys wouldn't of chucked turnips at you."

"How you figure all that?" Nathan asked. "That's crazy talk."

"Bible say, 'As a man sows, so shall he reap.' Y'all throwed rocks at the Germans, and God brought it back on you right away."

"You gone plumb crazy!" Nathan exclaimed. "I told you to shut up about that Bible stuff. You say one more word, I swear I'm gonna bust your head wide open."

"Let's just get home," I said.

"I told y'all not to go back to the camp after that guard

say for us to move along," Henry added. "If you'd of listened to me—"

That's when Nathan punched him in the stomach. Then he stalked off through the woods.

* * *

Pop was sitting on the porch when I came into the yard. "What on *earth* happen to you? Lucy!" he called. "Come out here."

I stood at the foot of the porch steps. Ma came through the door, wiping her hands on a dishtowel. "Caleb?" she exclaimed. "How—"

Pop got to his feet. "You been fightin'."

"Yes, sir."

Ma came toward me, but Pop stopped her.

"Frank, the boy's hurt. His lip's cut and that eye's a mess."

"Who'd you fight?" Pop demanded. "Don't tell me you and Nathan got into it."

"No, sir. He was with me, though. Henry, too."

"What happened?" Ma asked. Her voice was tight.

Now I was in for it. Wildly, I searched for a story—a lie—anything. Why hadn't I thought of something on the way home?

"He needs tending," Ma said.

"That can wait. Caleb, what'd you get into?"

There was no way out. I couldn't think of a lie, and

Pop could ask Nathan and Henry to check my story. "We went to the prison camp."

"What? That ain't no place for you!"

"Just to look at it. We went to the front gate and the guard told us to move."

"What else?"

"So we went around to the back of the camp—"

"After the guard told y'all to leave?"

"We were just standing there in the road, and he didn't have any right—"

Pop cut me off. "Yeah, he did! It his job to keep order around there."

"So we went around to the back and there were some prisoners playing soccer. We went up to the fence to watch them. They noticed us and one of them called us niggers."

"Oh, Lord," Ma cried.

Why had I said anything about that? Now the whole thing would come out. Might as well say it, because Henry would sure rat on me if Pop got to him.

"So Nathan and I got some rocks and threw them through the fence. I got one of them in the head."

Ma clapped her hand over her mouth.

"Jesus God!" Pop shouted. "You assaulted one of them POWs?"

"They called us niggers! We ran into the woods and started home."

"That still don't explain that lip and your eye. Tell me the truth, boy!"

Pop hadn't called me that in a long time.

"We were on the road, and the Hill brothers came up behind us on their wagon. I turned around to see who it was, and Dolan threw a turnip and got me right in the face. Then he got Henry in the head, too."

"Stinkin' white trash!" Pop exclaimed.

"We tried to walk away. Henry said we should, and we wanted to. But Lonnie told us not to turn our backs on him 'cause he's a white man."

"One of the nastiest, sorriest white boys on the face o' this earth."

"So we turned back, and Nathan said something that made Lonnie mad."

"That boy got a real big mouth," Pop noted bitterly.

"Then Lonnie said something else, and Nathan said something about Lonnie's mama, and then they jumped off the wagon and came after us. We had to fight, Pop!"

He looked serious. "How'd it turn out?"

"Nathan kicked Dolan between the legs—"

"Good for Nathan."

"And that laid him out, and then we fought off Lonnie and Orris. Orris got a bloody nose and Lonnie got a cut on his face."

"What about Nathan and Henry?" Ma asked. "They all right?"

"Nathan has a broken tooth and Henry's face is messed up some. They're okay."

"Sounds like you gave as good as you got," Pop remarked. "I'm glad about that, at least."

"We had to fight! We couldn't let them just beat us up."

"Let me take care of him," Ma said.

"Not yet. Caleb and me got some business to tend to in the workshop."

I knew what that meant. Pop intended to whip me. "No, Pop! I didn't do anything."

"Didn't *do* anything? You call goin' to that camp and messin' around with prisoners of the government not *doin'* anything? Do you know what kind of trouble you can get yourself into by foolin' with them Germans? And you call sassin' white folks not *doin'* anything?"

"Nathan sassed Lonnie, not me!"

"If y'all hadn't gone to where you wasn't suppose to be in the first place, you wouldn't of run into them crackers. Don't talk to me about not *doing* anything. Now get into the workshop."

"No! I'm too old for that."

"Hell you are! *I'm* the one who decide when one o' my boys is too old to get some sense beat into him. And you ain't got the sense of a tick!"

"No!" I said again. I could feel tears coming, but I blinked them back. There was no way I would cry in front of Pop.

He started down the steps toward me. "Git! Unless you ready to move out this evening and make it on your own from now on. 'Cause I ain't gonna put a roof over any child o' mine that won't obey me."

"Can't we talk about it?"

Pop folded his arms. "I gave you your choices. Now you decide, big man."

I looked toward Ma. She nodded.

It was done, then. I couldn't stand up against Ma. She had enough on her already.

"All right. You win."

"Go on. I be there in a minute."

I was standing by his workbench when he came in with his strap. "Pop, can't we—"

"You gonna go back on what we agreed?"

I didn't agree to anything, I thought. "No, sir."

"Then drop your britches."

"Not that!"

"Caleb?"

There was no way out. I'd lost. I unfastened my overalls and let them drop to my ankles. Please, not my drawers, too, I thought. If he insisted on whipping my bare backside, I'd run away. Even I had a limit.

But Pop didn't insist. "Turn around and put your hands on the bench."

I knew what to do. How many times had Randall and I taken our whippings this way?

"Now put your head down."

I obeyed.

The strap bit into my backside. It stung bad, and I fought to keep from making a sound. No way would I give Pop the satisfaction of hearing me cry out.

"Tell me you ain't gonna go down to that camp again."

"I won't."

"You won't *what?*"

"Go down to the camp again."

The strap cracked against me once more.

"Promise me you won't mess with white boys again."

I promised. Another lick. This time I flinched.

"Promise me you ain't gonna let that idiot Nathan lead you 'round by the nose. He gonna get hisself murdered one o' these days if he can't learn to shut up."

I promised, and the strap came again.

"And promise me that you ain't never, *ever* gonna talk back to me as long as you live!"

"I promise I won't ever talk back to you again."

Another stroke, this one harder than the others.

"Now turn 'round and apologize to me."

I made myself say the words, but I didn't mean them. If Pop intended to keep whipping me, I'd grab the strap and—

"Now drop them drawers," Pop ordered.

"Why—?"

He cut me off. "Didn't you just promise you wouldn't sass me?"

I could feel my hands wanting to move, not to take down my drawers, but to go after my own father. How—*how* had all this happened?

"Caleb!"

I turned back to the bench and pulled down my drawers.

"This didn't have to be, but I don't want to see you strung up on a tree one day. Don't you know by now that white folks'd just as soon kill you as look at you?"

"Yes, sir."

"I won't have many more chances to teach you that. Stay away from white folks, and when you got to be around 'em, keep yo' mouth shut! That the only way you ever gonna survive. Is that clear?"

"Yes, sir."

The next cut of the strap made me cry out. It stung more than any of the others.

"Last one," Pop said.

He didn't let up—this one seemed to cut into me like a knife.

"I hope you remember every word I told you in here. You might not believe me, but your life depends on it."

I kept my head down on the workbench so he couldn't see my tears.

"Now pull up your pants and get into the house. Your ma'll tend to you. I'm goin' over to talk to Henry's and

Nathan's folks. This is one hell of a mess you boys got your-
selves into."

When I knew he was gone, I let myself cry. My backside burned like fire, but that wasn't the reason. No, it was
the fury—fury deep down in my guts.

Before I went into the house, I swore I'd find a way to
get even with Pop. He couldn't use me like a dog and get
away with it.

CHAPTER SIX

MA HAD WARM WATER ready, and I had a bath while she waited in the front room. The water felt good, except on my backside. When I was done, she patched up my face and gave me some salve to put on the welts Pop's strap had raised.

Then I lay facedown on my bed. Looking at the empty bed next to mine suddenly made me miss Randall so bad that I started to cry again. *He* wouldn't have let Pop whip me. He'd have said something, done anything, to protect me.

I got up and lay down on Randall's bed. The quilt felt cool against my face. Where was he tonight, and what was he doing? Playing cards with his buddies in the barracks? In town somewhere, drinking and looking for girls? Or just lying on his bunk, thinking of home?

My brother was getting ready to go fight and kill— maybe *be* killed. *Life* magazine was full of pictures of the war in Europe and the Pacific. Our guys were getting slaughtered every day. Like Blaine Durden. And just down Brinson's Mill Road, prisoners that we'd captured were going to spend the rest of the war safe, playing soccer.

Why couldn't I be off with Randall? He was lucky to be old enough to join up and get away from Pop.

Ma came to the door. "Your daddy's back. Why are you on Randall's bed?"

I didn't know how to answer, but Ma seemed to understand. "Smooth out the quilt when you get up. Supper's on the table."

After Ma asked the blessing, Pop told us about going to Nathan's and Henry's. "No doubt where your buddy Nathan get his foolishness," he said. "Artie just laugh when I talk to him about the mess down at the camp and with them Hill boys. Course he already know what happen, 'cause Nathan show him his tooth, and anybody can see his face. And the whole time I'm tryin' to get Artie to see how serious this is, Nathan be addin' more details about what you boys said and done, and Artie think it the funniest damn thing he ever heard!"

Ma shook her head. "Artie has never been strict enough with Nathan."

"That ain't all. Artie say he *proud* of his boy for sassin' them Germans and for talkin' back to the Hill boys. Say he like to see a young man with some ball—some backbone!"

"What happened at the Johnsons'?" Ma asked.

"Just what you expect. Cora all to pieces about her precious baby boy gettin' hurt, fussin' over him like he five years old. Cecil actin' outraged at how Caleb and Nathan done led his boy into temptation, and about how the baptism sure ain't done no good—'specially for Nathan."

"How's Henry?" I asked.

"That little sissy make me sick! He start in on how he didn't want to go to the camp with y'all and how he try to get y'all to run into the woods when the Hills come along. He put all the blame on you and Nathan, which ain't no surprise."

Henry was telling the truth, mostly, but he made us look bad, trying to make himself look innocent.

"I suppose to give you a message," Pop told me.

"Who from?"

"From the *Reverend* Cecil Johnson."

"What is it?"

"That you and Nathan can't have nothin' more to do with Henry, 'cause you two is a bad influence on him. Henry ain't allowed to hang around with y'all, and he ain't gonna be workin' at Davis's with Nathan, either."

Suits me, I thought.

"I always said that boy is sorry."

"More stew?" Ma asked Pop. "Another biscuit?"

He poured syrup on his dinner. "So that's that. All we can do now is hope nothin' more come o' this thing. Looks like you got off easy, Caleb."

I kept my eyes on my plate.

"You do understand why you had to get that whippin'?"

I was silent.

"Maybe if Artie had laid the strap on Nathan when he little, Nathan wouldn't have that smart mouth on him now."

I kept my mouth shut, but it was hard. Pop didn't understand anything. He'd whipped Randall and me for years, but it hadn't made one bit of difference to how we behaved. I wasn't thinking about all his whippings when I threw the rock at the German, and I sure as hell wasn't thinking about them when the Hill boys came after us.

Sometimes you had to do what was necessary right then—no matter what bits of wisdom your folks had tried to cram into your brain.

* * *

As I tried to get to sleep that night, dark, ugly thoughts kept me company. I couldn't get comfortable. Usually I slept on my back, but my rear end hurt too much when I tried that, so I had to turn on my stomach, and that was worse. I settled for lying on my side.

Pop had no right to whip me. The more I thought about it, the madder I got. And I knew what I was going to do.

Next day, after my chores were done, I walked to The Cedars, Mr. Lee Davis's plantation. I expected that Aunt Lou, his cook, would answer the back door, but it was Aunt Minnie instead. Yes, Mr. Lee was at home, and she'd see if he would speak with me.

He came to the door, a fat, messy man in white linen trousers, white shirt, and a red necktie—the only outfit I'd ever seen him in. Mr. Davis greeted me with a hearty smile and asked about how my family was doing. Then he wanted to know all about Randall: where he was, how the training was going, and when he would be going overseas.

I answered all Mr. Davis's questions, saying "Yes, sir" and "No, sir" as I'd been taught, never looking the man in the eye. On the outside, I was polite, but inside, I would just as soon spit at him as beg him for work.

At last, Mr. Davis asked why I was there. It wouldn't do for me, or any Negro, to speak first. With eyes fixed on the dirt, I asked could I please work in his fields for the summer, now that Henry couldn't.

"Cecil come by this morning to tell me about that," Mr. Davis said. "He mentioned something about trouble Henry got into."

I wondered how much Brother Johnson had said, and whether he'd made Nathan and me look bad.

"Didn't say what the trouble was, and I didn't ask. None of my business, after all."

Mr. Davis didn't mean that. He made it his business to know everything going on within twenty miles of Davisville, but maybe he didn't think the troubles of some of his colored boys were worth knowing about.

I waited, like I had all the time in the world and the grass was the most interesting thing I'd ever seen.

"So you want to work here."

"Yes, sir."

"I thought you was goin' to work with your daddy."

I was ready for this. "I was goin' to, Mr. Lee, but Pop ain't gon' have as much work as he thought. 'Sides, I ain't a very good carpenter." I kept my voice low and humble, and I was careful not to use the proper grammar Ma had worked so hard to pound into me.

The man pulled out a crumpled white handkerchief and mopped his forehead. "I don't really need no extra help in the fields. Not with our new guests in town. You seen 'em yet?"

"You mean the prisoners, Mr. Lee?"

"That's right! I can't wait to see how they handle hoes and shovels. Hell of a lot better than the rifles they was aiming at our boys in Africa, the goddamn Nazi sons of bitches."

I said nothing, just kept my eyes on my shoes.

"You really do need a job?" he asked doubtfully.

"Oh, yes, sir. Especially now that Randall gone."

"That's true. We don't want your family to go through hard times because your brother is off serving his country. That wouldn't be fair, now, would it?"

"No, sir. I reckon not."

"Tell you what. The Dixie Belle already looks like it's gonna be a big success. I'm half owner, you know."

"I heard that, Mr. Lee."

"That place is a gold mine! Even with a war on, folks got to eat."

Where was he going with this?

"How'd you like a job in the kitchen? Lou told me just last evening that they can use a boy to wash dishes. Think that's something you could do?"

Now I was sorry I'd come. The last thing in the world I wanted to do was work at the Dixie Belle. But it was too late to say no. You never refused a white man's offer—not if you knew what was good for you.

"It'd be hard work," he warned. "Hot, too, with summer comin' on, and all that boilin' grease for the chicken heatin' up the kitchen even more. Think you could handle it?"

There was no choice. "I think I could, Mr. Lee. Thank you for offerin' it to me."

"I can pay you same as my field hands get—ten cents an hour."

"Thank you, sir."

"Can you start tomorrow? Say at six? We open for breakfast at seven, and there's work to do before that."

Not even Mr. Davis's field hands had to be on the job that early, and Pop never left the house to go to a job until after seven. Working with him suddenly looked like heaven compared to this.

But I was trapped. "I can start tomorrow, Mr. Lee."

"You got to work hard. If you don't, I can't keep you on. Understand?"

"Yes, sir."

"All right, then. Report at six. You'll work until three, after dinner is all cleaned up. We ain't open in the evenings—yet. Agreed?"

"Yes, sir. And thank you, sir."

He beamed at me. Mr. Lee Davis was never happier than when he was doing nice and generous things for "his Negroes." I nodded and thanked him again, and stood and waited while he went back inside. Negroes never walked away from whites. We waited until they left us, and then we were free to go back to our own business.

My business right now was spitting in Mrs. Davis's flower bed and figuring out how to break my news to Pop.

* * *

I planned to tell him right before supper. If he got crazy mad and wanted to whip me again, I'd leave home, no matter how Ma felt about it.

Pop was at the pump, washing up. "How you?" he asked.

"Enjoy your last day o' freedom? I'm ready to put you to work tomorrow. Got a couple big jobs comin' up."

This was it. "Pop, I'm not gonna work with you this summer after all."

He stopped drying his face and looked at me like he hadn't heard right. "What you talkin' about? Course you gonna work with me this summer. We planned it weeks ago."

My insides felt all shaky. "I changed my mind. Today I went over to Mr. Davis's place and asked him to give me a job. I start at the Dixie Belle Café tomorrow, as a dishwasher."

For a moment, Pop looked blank. Then he smirked. "Oh, I get it. This all about you gettin' whipped, ain't it? You got yo' feelin's all hurt, and now you gonna get back at the old man. You gonna teach *me* a lesson. *I'm* gonna pay now, right?"

"That's not it, Pop," I lied. "It'll be better if we're not around each other all day. I just make you mad. You can find a better helper."

"Damn right I can! I was gonna do you a favor, let you come work with me, learn a few things about hammer and nails. You need some lessons, Caleb, 'cause you ain't much of a carpenter—and that God's truth. I thought maybe you'd like to learn somethin' from me. But you the big man now, so suit yourself."

His words stung because they were true. Carpentry and me didn't get along, and I envied Randall when Pop praised his skills with a hammer and saw.

"Get washed up and come on to supper. I reckon you can't wait to crow about this in front of your ma."

"Pop—"

"There ain't nothin' more to say. You made your choice. It ain't no skin off my back. If I can find a helper, fine. If not, no matter. I can work faster and better without always havin' to show someone like you what to do."

That hurt, too.

"I'm goin' in. If you intend to eat, wash up and come on."

He threw the damp towel at me and went into the house.

There hadn't been a shouting match. Pop hadn't made a move to punish me. I'd gotten my way. I'd won.

But it didn't feel like much of a victory.

CHAPTER SEVEN

T HAT NIGHT I kept waking up, sure it was morning and I'd overslept. The first time, the clock in the sitting room said one thirty. Then three. At five twenty I got up. When I came back from the outhouse, Ma was stirring up the fire.

"Morning, hon. You finish getting ready and I'll have something for you to eat in a few minutes. You reckon you'll need a dinner, too?"

"Gosh, Ma. You didn't have to get up."

"A man needs something in his belly before he goes out the door. I'll fry you up a couple eggs in no time."

Neither of us heard Pop coming. "No, you ain't gonna

fry him up no eggs," he announced from the doorway. We both jumped at the sound of his voice. "Lucy, you work from dawn to night every day, takin' care o' this family, and I ain't gonna have you wakin' up in the pitch dark to feed this boy no early breakfast. If Caleb need to be on his way this early, he can look out for hisself."

"Frank, he can't go to work hungry."

"If he was doin' what he promised he'd be doin' this summer, he wouldn't have to go hungry. But seein' how he makin' his own decisions an' all, he jus' gonna have to look out for hisself. Now you come on back to bed."

"You're not being fair. He needs something to eat."

"He goin' to a restaurant, ain't he? Let *them* give him his breakfast. Wish I could eat at the fanciest place in town every morning."

"There's no reason to be ugly."

I felt plenty angry now. "Never mind, Ma. Pop's right. I don't need anything."

"Can he at least fix himself something?" Ma asked.

Pop shrugged. "Long as he quiet and clean up after hisself. I ain't gonna have him wakin' us up before we got to be on our feet, and I sure as hell ain't gonna have him make no extra work for you."

"How thoughtful." Ma's sarcasm was obvious.

"I have to go," I said. "Before I'm late."

Pop moved to let me pass. Now I was sore. He was being

as mean as he could, just to get back at me. Well, I could play that game, too.

In a minute I was ready to leave. Pop had gone back to bed—he wouldn't even say goodbye.

Ma slipped a cold yam in my pocket. "Your father will calm down in a couple days," she promised. "And I'll make sure there's always something for you to take, even if I can't cook for you in the mornings."

"Thanks, Ma." I let her hug me.

"Do your best," she called after me as I left the yard. "I'm proud of you, Caleb."

I hoped Pop had heard that from his bed.

* * *

The road to Davisville took me through some woods. Although light was growing in the sky, here it was all dark and shadowy. I stopped and waited, straining my ears. Somewhere, far off, a whippoorwill called. High above me, two nighthawks squawked, looking for a few last bugs before roosting for the day. And in the distance, probably miles away, a train sounded its whistle.

"God?" I said.

No reply.

"You there?"

Silence, except for the cries of the nighthawks.

"I believe in you, I really do. And I promise I'll do what you want, but I need for you to tell me what that is. Please!"

I waited humbly, the way Brother Johnson said we had to come before the Throne of Grace.

But there was no answer, and I couldn't be late on my first day of work. In fact I ran the rest of the way, just to make sure I'd be on time.

Davisville was still dark as I walked toward the square. There were lights in the Dixie Belle, though, and I could smell bacon frying.

I was surprised when Uncle Hiram met me at the back door. "What are you doing here, Uncle Hiram?" I asked. He'd worked at the Davises' for years, doing all kinds of handyman work around their place, just like Aunt Lou had been their cook ever since anyone could remember.

"Ain't you heard? Mr. Lee done promoted Lou and me. She the head cook at the Dixie Belle now, an' I's her number one assistant."

I felt a lot better. Working with folks I knew—and who knew and liked me—would make this job a lot easier.

"Come on in," he told me. "Mist' Lee say you be comin' on board. I's glad, too. Already done had my fill o' washin' dishes."

"Mornin', sugar," Aunt Lou called. She was at a big table, rolling out biscuits. "Hiram an' me is mighty glad to see you. We can use every pair o' hands. You hungry?"

"Yes, ma'am!"

"If you can wait jes' a little, I soon have some hot

biscuits for you. Now take yo' time and look over the place. Better do it while you can, 'cause it gon' be mighty busy in a little while."

"I can show him," Uncle Hiram volunteered.

"Stir them grits when you go by the stove," said Aunt Lou.

Uncle Hiram took me around and explained my work. Wash dishes, scrub pots and pans, dry and put them away, clean vegetables, peel potatoes, take out the garbage, tidy the dining room, mop the kitchen at the end of every day . . .

All for ten cents an hour.

I realized what a mess I was in—and that I'd done it to myself. Working with Pop, for the same pay, would be a hundred times easier. I was ready to tell Uncle Hiram I'd changed my mind.

I could quit and make up some excuse to give Mr. Davis. But go back and apologize to Pop? Ask if he'd still take me on as his helper? Hell, no! Not after he'd whipped me. Not after the way he'd acted this morning.

"Where do I start?" I asked.

Aunt Lou put biscuits on a baking sheet. "You can scrub them collards. After that batch we got in here Sunday, we better wash everythin' extra good."

"What was wrong with the collards?" There was no way Aunt Lou could know what Nathan and I had done, was there?

"Don't know, exactly. But they smelled awful! Taters, too."

"Did you cook them anyway?"

"After we done washed 'em good. They was all right in the end, but you can't never be too careful. Ain't that right?"

I smiled. "Yes, ma'am. It sure is."

* * *

While Aunt Lou fried bacon, fatback, and sausage, stirred the grits, and baked biscuits, Uncle Hiram did his work, and I washed collards and peeled potatoes. At six forty-five, the waitresses arrived. Voncille—I knew to call her Miss Voncille—was an older white woman with dyed red hair, pencil-thin eyebrows, and too much pink lipstick. She came in, grabbed an apron, tied it over her green uniform dress, and said not a word when Uncle Hiram introduced me. She helped herself to black coffee from the big urn by the door and started filling up glass coffeepots, which she carried into the dining room.

The other waitress was a white girl named Betty Jean. She wasn't a whole lot older than me, maybe Randall's age, but I'd be calling her Miss Betty Jean even so. She looked like a country girl, but she was pretty. And at least she said hey.

Just before seven, Sondra Davis made her grand entrance. She was married to Mr. Lee Davis's little brother, James Ewell, and she had a reputation. Everyone knew how she'd caught her first husband in bed with another woman and thrown him out that very night. Miss Sondra got everything he had. The day her divorce came through, she married James Ewell and then went behind his back and got Mr. Lee to go in with her and start the Dixie Belle. Miss Sondra was one tough cookie.

"Miz Sondra, you shore do look purty this mornin'," Uncle Hiram told her as she got herself some coffee. She ignored him and helped herself to a warm biscuit. "This be the new boy," he went on. "Frank Brown boy, Caleb. You might of seed him around."

She glanced at me and then gave her attention to the syrup pitcher. "Lee had no business hiring anyone without asking me," she complained. "I told him it's too soon to know if we need anyone else."

"We couldn't keep up good over the weekend. It got right backed up in here durin' Sunday dinner. Last two days been busy, too. You know how it was."

"Only because we haven't gotten organized yet! If Lee could just be patient, he'd see that you and Aunt Lou can handle things."

Aunt Lou rolled biscuits like she wanted to squash them flat.

"Caleb do good for you, Miz Sondra. He a strong, honest, reliable boy."

I was glad Pop couldn't hear Uncle Hiram talk about

me that way. Pop would laugh at me for begging a job where even the other Negroes called me "boy" in front of the white folks.

Miss Sondra eyed me like she was inspecting a hog she might buy. "He looks all right. But understand," she said, "I expect you to *work* for your pay. Got that?"

"Yes, ma'am. I do a good job for you."

"See that you do. I can't afford to pay lazy people."

It had taken the woman only a minute to make me hate her.

Miss Voncille poked her head through the door. "It's seven, and folks are waitin' to come in. You want me to open up?"

"All right. Is everything ready, Lou?"

"Ready as it gonna be. Let 'em come on."

"Go ahead, then," Miss Sondra said. "Let's see how it goes this morning."

I heard the front door being unlocked, then voices. My first day had officially begun.

*　*　*

For the next three hours, the work never stopped. Voncille and Betty Jean kept bringing dirty plates through the door and dumping them on the sink. Soon, the sight of rubbery cold grits, sticky egg yolks, and bits of half-eaten pork made me tired—and a little sick. Some people even stubbed out their cigarettes in their food and left the butts on the plate. It was my job to separate food from paper napkins, cigarettes, and anything else Mr. Davis's hogs shouldn't eat.

Right away, Voncille decided I was her personal boy. And that's what she called me, too. "Boy, I need more forks right now." "You got to keep the clean coffee cups comin', boy." "If you intend to keep workin' here, you best step it up, boy." She never thanked me. Hell, she never looked at me.

"Try not to mind her," Aunt Lou whispered to me after Voncille had snapped at me for handing her a wet saucer. "She ain't nothin' but white trash without the manners God give a mule."

But I did mind her.

I was sweating as I bent over the sink, which was too low for me, and my back started to ache. Clean plates, glasses, coffee cups, and silverware piled up in the drainers. Whenever there was a free second, I had to dry them and stack them on shelves by the griddle. Tomorrow I'd bring a head rag and some rubber gloves—if there was a tomorrow. The thought of quitting kept coming back, and I kept shooing it away. Quitting after one day would be worse than doing it before I ever got started. If I didn't come back tomorrow, Pop would say it was because I couldn't take it. No way I'd give him that satisfaction.

By ten the breakfast rush was over. Plates of cold food

stopped showing up on the sink, and there was no more to scrape into the garbage cans. At last everything was caught up—for a while. Aunt Lou inspected my work and said I'd done a good job. "Let's take a break," she said. "Caleb, you ready for your breakfast?"

I said I could eat one of the plates, I was so hungry.

"Come on, then. I cook you something. How you like yo' eggs?"

Aunt Lou cooked me three, sunny-side up, and I was trying not to gobble them when Miss Sondra came into the kitchen. She looked at me and frowned.

"We had no agreement about this boy eating here. Why didn't you ask me first, Aunt Lou?"

"Caleb done work hard all mornin'. I reckon he earned hisself a plate o' food."

"I don't believe it's customary for restaurants to feed their employees for free. He can get himself something before he comes to work. There's a war on, and I can't afford charity."

I put my fork down and looked at my breakfast. Everything tasted like poison now. She could keep her precious food. I pushed the plate away.

Aunt Lou looked annoyed, but she kept her temper. "He got to leave the house mighty early. No time to get no hot meal."

"That's his problem, not mine."

"You mind if I feed him dinner? What he eat wouldn't be nothin' compare to what folks be wastin'."

"Those two things have nothing to do with each other! If he wants to eat his dinner here, he can pay for it, like everyone else. I'm willing to be fair: fifteen cents a day for his dinner. Fifteen more if he wants his breakfast." She looked at her wristwatch. "I'm late for my beauty appointment. I'll be back in an hour. You know what to do to get dinner finished."

"Yes, ma'am."

When she was gone, Aunt Lou told Uncle Hiram exactly what she thought about that high-and-mighty Sondra Davis, who wasn't anything better than a backcountry cracker and a gold digger to boot, who had most likely been making time with Mr. James Ewell all those nights her husband was shacking up with his harlot. She said Miss Sondra had her claws so deep into Mr. James Ewell now, he'd never get rid of her, and she bet he was sorry he'd married such a hussy.

I enjoyed every word.

"I know it ain't Christian for me to talk like I do," Aunt Lou went on, "but sometimes I think God done put the Davis family on this earth jus' to test my faith. If that woman don't lay off, I'm gon' to be gone from here real soon. *Real* soon! Didn't want to come over here anyway. I belong back in my own kitchen at Mr. Lee place! I's a fool to let him sweet-talk me into comin' over here. I ain't no restaurant cook. Five days—only five days!—and I already done had enough."

Uncle Hiram put his arm around her shoulder. "Come on, now, sugar. Don't let that woman upset you. She ain't worth a drop o' yo' spit, and that God's truth."

"Sayin' that Caleb got to pay for his meals! Three hours' pay for a breakfast and a dinner? No way! Don't you worry," she told me. "I's gon' feed you, and that tight-fisted bitch ain't never got to know one thing about it."

"How, Aunt Lou?"

"She can't be in here every minute, can she? Not as long as she havin' so much fun playin' hostess. What she don't know won't hurt her."

"What about the waitresses? They come in here all the time."

"I can feed you outside the back door if I got to! Both of them stuck-up white ladies too good to go back there with the colored help."

I had to smile again. Maybe things wouldn't be so bad after all. Not with Aunt Lou on my side.

* * *

While Aunt Lou worked on dinner, I was sent into the dining room to sweep and tidy up. The room was empty, the front door locked, and a Closed sign faced the sidewalk. I felt nervous, like I was trespassing. Any second I expected some invisible white person to tell me to get out.

Voncille and Betty Jean had left me the tables to clean,

even though that was supposed to be their job. The ashtrays were full. The floor was littered and some wet, sticky places needed mopping. I hadn't made any of this mess, but it was my job to clean it up. Ma said she wondered why so many Negroes spent their lives picking up after white folks. Now I truly understood what she meant.

While I worked, good smells got my mouth watering. By half past eleven, when the Dixie Belle opened for dinner, Aunt Lou and Uncle Hiram had put together a menu of fried chicken, pork chops, mashed potatoes or rice with gravy, macaroni and cheese, collards, squash casserole, black-eyed peas, and pans of cornbread. For dessert there was banana pudding or lemon icebox pie.

If I thought breakfast was busy, dinner was crazy. And it lasted just as long. I had my arms in my third sinkful of hot, soapy water when Mr. Davis burst into the kitchen. His son, Stewart, a handsome, blond-haired guy Randall's age, was right behind him.

"How y'all doing in here today?" said Mr. Davis. "Lou, you all right?"

"Yessuh." She didn't even look up from her skillet of pork chops.

"Caleb, how's it going?"

"Just fine, sir."

"They keepin' you busy?"

I grinned at him. "Yes, sir!"

"I knew they would! Aunt Lou knows how to crack the whip."

Stewart Davis broke in. "Where's that lemon pie?"

Aunt Lou nodded toward the refrigerator.

"And a plate?"

"On that shelf over yonder."

"What about a knife?"

"Somebody cut Mr. Stewart a piece of that pie."

Uncle Hiram got a knife and fork, but Stewart insisted on cutting his own piece—one big enough for three people. "No one makes lemon pie as good as you, Aunt Lou," he exclaimed through a mouthful. "I can't forgive Daddy for lettin' you come work here. We sure do miss you back at the house."

"You best take that up with him."

"Lou, we've been over this," Mr. Davis said. "It don't have to be forever. Just help Sondra and me get started. One thing for sure: we got ourselves some satisfied customers out there. Folks say they can't get chicken good as yours anywhere around here, not even up in Augusta."

"Them's mighty fine words, Mr. Lee, but please understand one thing. We *got* to have another cook, and that's a fact. Hiram and me is too old to keep up this pace. Either you find me some more help, or we both gon' quit. You let Miz Sondra know that, too. Now I got to watch these pork chops so's they don't burn."

"Fry a couple real crisp for me," Stewart said. "You know I like mine extra brown." He put down his pie plate and tried to hug her.

Aunt Lou shrugged him off. "I ain't got no time for no foolishness! I can take care o' yo' pork chops, but you got to let me be."

"I'm goin' back into the dining room," Davis said. "Come on, son."

"You be sure to tell Miz Sondra what I said," Aunt Lou called after him.

"She won't want to pay for more help," Stewart said after his father was gone. "Aunt Sondra likes to stretch a dollar."

He started to pinch off some of the crusty top from a pan of macaroni and cheese, but Aunt Lou swatted his hand away. "Quit that! Folks don't want to eat nothin' after you got your grubby fingers in it. We ain't back at the house."

"Oh, all right. I'll go keep Daddy company. Have one of the girls bring out the pork chops when they're ready."

"Anything to get you outta here! I got more to do than I can manage."

I kept my eyes on the dirty plates in the sink. Betty Jean brought another load and dumped them on the counter.

"Looks like you got more than you can manage, too!" Stewart joked. "Look sharp, now!"

He went into the dining room. I had some ideas what

to do with his pork chops before Aunt Lou sent them out to him, but it wasn't my place to say anything. No, my place was to scrub pans clean from macaroni and cheese, where the cheese had baked on to the metal and had to be worked free with a wire brush.

While I washed and rinsed, Aunt Lou's ways with the white folks kept coming into my mind. She was respectful to Mr. Davis, but she talked to Stewart like he was one of her own grandchildren. And Stewart obeyed her, too. Not many Negroes I knew could talk to whites the way Aunt Lou did. I figured she'd earned it by all the years of what Lee Davis would call "faithful service" to his family. I knew that meant getting up in the dark to be at the Davis kitchen in time to put a hot breakfast on the table every morning, even Sundays. It meant staying late in the evenings to clear the table and wash the dishes while the white folks socialized and called for more coffee and dessert. It meant a lifetime of scraping dirty plates, scrubbing dirty pots, and drying and putting everything away at night so the whole mess could start over again next morning.

"Behold my servant." I saw Aunt Lou wipe the sweat off her face while she tended to Stewart's frying pork chops. She and Uncle Hiram had spent their whole lives serving white folks. And for what? I wanted something different for myself. Something better. If God was calling me to be his servant, surely that didn't mean spending my life waiting on white people.

Toward the end of the dinner shift, Miss Sondra came in and started wrangling with Aunt Lou about getting a second cook. Miss Sondra argued that things would get easier and that money was tight, but Aunt Lou held on. Either they found another helper, or she and Uncle Hiram were leaving. If nothing changed within a week, they'd be gone, and Miss Sondra could stand by a hot stove herself and see how she liked it.

Four o'clock came and went before my work was done. The dining room was swept, everything in the kitchen washed, the garbage hauled to the alley, and the kitchen mopped. Aunt Lou told me again what a help I'd been. That made me feel good.

On my way home, I thought some more about how Aunt Lou broke the rules I'd heard all my life. "Never let a white person see you angry or upset." "Never threaten a white person." "Do what a white person says without asking why." She had earned the right to disobey those rules. And she had paid a lot for that right, as far as I could tell.

* * *

At home, Ma was working on supper. "How was your day?" she asked. "Was it hard? You look tuckered out."

She sounded so sympathetic that I told her the truth. "Awful. It's hot, the sink is too low, and my back is killing me. Miss Sondra is rude, and so is one of the waitresses."

"I'm sorry. You could quit and go back with your father."

"Not a chance. You saw how he was this morning."

Ma sighed, then brightened up. "A letter from Randall arrived today. Guess what? He's coming home on leave soon."

"Does Pop know?"

"Not yet. Take care of your chores, and then you can wash up and rest."

I started to go, but Ma called after me, "Remember that your father is a stubborn man. He can hold out a long time."

"I'll remember, Ma."

Like I could ever forget.

Over supper, Pop told us about his day, and then he and Ma discussed when Randall might be home and what we'd do during his visit. Of course Pop didn't ask about *my* day—that was part of my punishment.

I waited until he had a mouth full of field peas. "I had a busy day, too, Pop."

"So?"

"Aunt Lou said I did a good job."

"Huh."

"She and Uncle Hiram are gonna quit unless Mr. Lee hires more help."

"That ain't no concern o' mine. The man can hire a hundred more slaves if he want to. Or burn the place down. It don't matter a bit to me."

"Look, Pop. I'm sorry I hurt your feelings."

Pop looked up from his plate. "Hurt my feelings? Is that what you think?"

"I don't know. Why can't you be glad I got my own job?"

He put down his fork. "You call washin' dishes for the white folks a *job?* That ain't nothin' but nigger work! You don't make nothin', you don't learn nothin', and you don't count for nothin'."

"I've washed plenty of dishes for them in my time," Ma noted. "Was that 'nigger work'? All those clean dishes helped put food on this table."

"That different! Ain't no other kind o' work for Negro womens. You had to do it, and I'm thankful you did. But Caleb here—he had a choice, and he made a bad one. Ain't nothin' more to say."

Enough was enough. I jumped up from the table and headed for the front door. If I didn't get out of there, I'd end up yelling at Pop, and that wouldn't end well.

I threw open the door.

And there was Randall.

CHAPTER EIGHT

Hey, LITTLE BROTHER!" he exclaimed, grabbing my shoulders. "Where you goin' in such a big hurry?"

I pulled the door shut behind me, too surprised to speak.

"What'sa matter? This any way to welcome a soldier?"

"What are you doing here?" I managed to ask.

"I live here!"

"Ma got your letter today. We didn't expect you so quick."

"I thought I'd surprise y'all. Looks like I have."

I took a deep breath. "Oh, man, it's good to see you."

"Something wrong?"

"Pop and I are fighting."

"Just like always. What about?"

"Later. Come on. They'll want to see you."

Randall grinned. "Listen! You go back in and tell 'em you got something for 'em to see out here."

"Okay."

In the kitchen, Ma was pouring Pop some coffee.

"Y'all come to the porch."

"Why?" Ma asked.

"Somebody wants to see you."

"Who?"

"I don't know, but he says it's important."

"From the army? I pray nothing's wrong."

Now I felt bad. I hadn't meant to scare her.

"What's all this?" Pop asked.

"Nothing bad. Just come on."

Ma let out a little scream when she saw Randall, and then she had her arms around his neck. "You should have told us you were coming tonight," she exclaimed. "We only got your letter today."

"I wanted to surprise you. When they gave us leave so quick, I decided to come on."

"How you get here?" Pop asked.

"Train to Augusta, then down to Waynesboro, then hitched a ride with a white guy taking a load of furniture to Savannah."

"That was kind of him," Ma said.

"He was all right. Said he was glad to help a fellow in uniform."

"Of course he was. Oh, let me look at you, son. My goodness, you're handsome! And haven't you put on some weight?"

"Twelve pounds."

"You do look good," Pop agreed. "Come in the house and your ma'll fix you somethin' to eat. How long you gonna be home?"

"Ten days."

"Caleb, get your brother's duffle bag." Pop didn't even look at me.

"I still wish I'd known you were coming," Ma was saying. "I could have fried up a chicken. Well, tomorrow . . ."

They went inside, and there I was, alone. It was great having Randall home, but for the next ten days, the world would center on him. I was the second son, left to tote my big brother's bag.

Ma heated up what was left of supper, fried some fatback and eggs, and opened a jar of peaches she'd put up in the summer. It was the last one, and she'd been saving it for a special occasion.

Randall went at it like he was starving, and they watched him like they'd never seen anyone eat before. Ma chattered about the Toad Hop news, and Pop put in his ten cents' worth about crops, the weather, and his latest jobs. Randall let them talk.

Ma bustled about, refilling his plate. "Don't they feed you?" she asked. "You want some more eggs?"

"They gotta be feedin' the boy *somethin'*, Lucy. Look at how much he done filled out."

"Basic training," Randall explained. "All the bread and potatoes you can eat, and ten thousand pushups."

"They treat you all right?" Pop asked. "You Negroes?"

Randall hesitated. "About what I expected. A few of the officers are okay, but most of 'em are dedicated racists. We made up a joke about 'em. Want to hear it?"

"If it ain't indecent."

"What do you get when you put a redneck in an officer's uniform?... A guy in the best suit of clothes he ever owned!"

Pop laughed. Ma looked doubtful.

Pop got serious again. "If they ain't treatin' you right, you oughta say somethin'."

"Aw, Pop, you know better than that. Who we gonna complain to—General Patton?"

"So ain't nothin' changed. They grab up all the Negroes they can lay they hands on and send 'em to fight and die. And all the time, they treat 'em like shit."

Only a day or so ago, Pop had been complaining that Negro soldiers *wouldn't* get a chance to fight.

"Country asks our boys to put they lives on the line, but won't treat 'em like citizens."

"It's mostly all right," Randall said. "They work us hard, but we can see the white boys getting their share, too. And I made me some solid friends, guys I know I can count on, no matter what."

"All Negroes, I bet."

Randall laughed. "Who else? They ain't any white boys in our company."

"Welcome to the Jim Crow Army!" Pop exclaimed.

"Let's talk about something else," Ma suggested.

"Sorry, Ma. I'll be all right. Nothin' can happen to me. I can count on my buddies, too."

We chatted some more. Randall didn't ask me about what I was doing, and I was glad. He didn't have a chance, really, not while Pop was drilling him with more questions about his training.

Finally Randall said he was beat and had to hit the bed. He hadn't slept in thirty-six hours.

"Your bed's all made up," Ma said. "Caleb, get your brother a towel."

"Let me help with the dishes first," Randall offered.

"Not on your life! Caleb can help me. It's early yet."

I sure didn't feel like doing any more dishes. I wanted to talk to my brother, just the two of us, but that would have to wait.

When I went to the bedroom at ten, I expected Randall to be asleep, but he was awake, lying on top of his covers, arms crossed behind his head. He'd undressed down to his underwear.

"Hey, man. I thought you'd be long gone," I said.

"Shhh. Close the door."

I did, then sat on my bed. "What's wrong?"

"Can't settle down. I need sleep bad, but my brain won't give me any peace."

"You scared of going over there?" The second I said that, I wished I hadn't.

But he wasn't bothered. "Damn right I'm scared! All the guys are. Even the ones who won't admit it."

"I'd be shaking. There's a lot of killing. Real bad stuff, from what the papers say." I wished I hadn't said that, either.

"That's only part of it. I'm worried we're gonna get over there and mess up."

"Mess up? How?"

"Not be good soldiers. Get so scared we can't fight. Turn yellow and run like little boys. That's just what some of the big shots think we'll do, anyway."

"Your officers? They wouldn't think that."

Randall turned toward me. "Like hell! Some of the generals don't even want us to have guns. They think all we're good for is diggin' ditches and loadin' freight. We been treated like dirt the whole time."

"You said some of the officers are okay."

"A couple, but they don't make up for the rest. There's a bunch of stuff I could of said, but I don't want to get Pop all riled up, or worry Ma."

"How do they treat you bad?"

"Every way they can! Like a drill sergeant callin' us a 'bunch of dumb niggers' when we had trouble on an obstacle course. Or being harassed by white policemen in Louisiana every time we left camp to go into town. And the white MPs takin' their side!"

Randall got quiet. I waited.

"The worst was somethin' I overheard at Huachuca, over in Arizona. I was doin' some cleanup in an office and some officers was in the next room, talkin'. 'I don't care how you dress 'em up,' this one guy says. 'A coon's a coon, even in uniform. You can't trust 'em any further than you can kick 'em.' I almost went AWOL that night, but figured it wasn't worth doin' time in the stockade."

I wished I could tell Randall not to go back. But they'd track him down and put him in prison.

"What were y'all fightin' about when I got here?"

I told him, ending with my day at the Dixie Belle. As I hoped he would, he took my side. He was especially mad about Pop whipping me. "He always been way too free with that damn strap. Somebody should of told him years ago it never done any good."

"You got it a lot more than me."

"Don't I know it! Didn't stop me from doin' anything, though—just made me better at keepin' things a secret."

"He won't ever whip me again," I vowed. "I'll leave first."

"I wouldn't blame you. Hey, you been goin' out any?"

"Some. I was thinking of going out tonight, maybe see Nathan."

"You'll have to climb over me to do it."

"I know."

"If you do, watch where you put your feet." He was laughing.

I promised I'd be careful. Then I told him about the last time we went out, and about sneaking some of Mr. Artie's 'shine, and about what Nathan and me did at the Dixie Belle. He laughed hard at that and said he was glad we'd done it. "And you ain't ever gotten caught yet," he added. "Somebody taught you real good."

"Maybe we can go out together while you're home. The two of us, just like we used to."

"Sure. I'd like that. What else you been into lately, besides fightin' with the old man and gettin' an honest job?"

Here was my chance to tell my brother the most important thing. Now was as good a time as any. "I got baptized last Sunday, and something strange happened that day. I wanted to write it to you, but you wouldn't have gotten my letter anyway."

He was quiet, like he was waiting for me to continue.

I told him about the voice, and what it had said, and how I figured it was God. I kept waiting for him to say something, even to laugh at me, but there was only his slow, soft breathing. My brother had fallen asleep while I was still talking.

CHAPTER NINE

CALEB, TIME TO GET UP. You don't want to be late."

I opened my eyes and there was Ma, standing over my bed. "Be quiet so you don't wake your brother."

Randall lay facing the wall, the covers pulled over his head.

"I got you a clean shirt in the kitchen. Come on, now."

When my feet were on the floor, I realized my back ached. Go to work again? No, thanks. But I had to. My plans to go out and see Nathan hadn't happened, either. I was just too beat.

Ma had clean socks for me as well as a shirt and a

bandanna for my head. She put a paper bag and some money in my hand. "A little breakfast. You can eat while you walk. If you get a minute later on, buy yourself some rubber gloves."

"Gee, thanks, Ma."

"Mothers do what they can."

Pop was nowhere around. Still in bed, most likely.

I munched a cold biscuit with bacon on my way. Uncle Hiram would have the coffee ready, strong and hot. Good thing. I needed it.

When I came to the woods, I stopped, just like I had the day before. And listened. This morning even the birds were silent.

I felt shy about talking out loud, but no one was around, and I had nothing to lose. "God, I'm here. It's Caleb. You have anything to say to me?"

Nothing.

"That's okay," I told him. "I can wait. When you're ready, you'll talk to me. But how can I serve you until I know what you want me to do?"

I went on my way feeling better than I had in a few days.

My second day at the Dixie Belle was easier in some ways, harder in others. It wasn't all new and strange, but my back hurt and I didn't want to be there. And Voncille didn't let up. She told Sondra Davis, right in front of me,

"I sure hope you can find some help that can work faster than this boy." What made some white folks think all Negroes were deaf?

At dinnertime Mr. Davis and Stewart barged into the kitchen again. Mr. Davis tried to sweet-talk Aunt Lou, but she repeated how he had better get her that second cook. He promised, then went into the dining room to eat.

Stewart poked his nose into things and got in the way. Just before they came in, Aunt Lou had taken a big metal pan of peach cobbler out of the oven and set it on the work table to cool. He asked for some, but she told him she was too busy, that he was in her way and to wait a minute, so he decided to help himself. He picked up the pan, which was still burning hot, shouted, and dropped it on the edge of the table. From there, it smashed to the floor. Hot syrup splattered everywhere, including on Aunt Lou's legs.

What a prize jackass, I thought.

Stewart understood my expression exactly. "What the hell are you lookin' at? Can't you see there's a mess to clean up? Get over here and take care of it. And in the future, keep your damn eyes where they belong, if you want to keep your job."

What I wanted was to put my fist in his face.

He gave me a dirty look and stalked out, leaving Uncle Hiram to get Aunt Lou calmed down and me to scrape up the sticky mess from the floor. Twenty minutes later, Mr.

Davis came in and listened while Aunt Lou told him just what she thought about his son's behavior and how she was one step closer to walking out for good. She'd saved her pennies and was ready to retire anyway.

It surprised me to hear Mr. Davis apologize for Stewart. From my place at the sink, I saw him put some bills in Aunt Lou's apron pocket. He said he'd "handle" everything and vowed his son would apologize, too.

* * *

I came into the yard that afternoon and found Randall on the porch. He asked about my day, so I told him about Voncille, and he said what did I expect from an ignorant white-trash woman? When I mentioned Stewart Davis's name, though, he got mad. "Draft-dodging son of a bitch! He was up at Gordon same day as I was, for our physicals. He's every bit as healthy as me, but he got to come right on back home to daddy, while I got a ticket to Germany."

Ma came to the door. "Caleb, honey, I want to hear all about your day, but there's so much to do. Please take care of your outside chores, and then you can tell me everything while we work in the kitchen." More chores were the last thing I felt like doing.

When the wood was chopped, the chickens fed, and Sweetie's stall mucked out, I reported for kitchen duty. Two pies sat on the warmer, and the room smelled of simmering greens. For the next hour, I worked as hard as I had at the Dixie Belle. I didn't make ten cents, but no one would grudge me my supper.

While we ate, Randall kept us laughing with stories about the crazy GIs he'd met and the messes they'd gotten themselves into. But when he'd enjoyed his third piece of pecan pie and finished his fourth cup of coffee, Randall got serious.

"When I was at Huachuca, I met this guy from Atlanta, name of Sonny Jones. Looks like we're shippin' out together. Good guy—someone I can trust."

"In the army, all you can count on is your buddies," Pop said. "I learned that real fast."

"Anyway, like I said, Sonny's from Atlanta, where his daddy owns a business—contracting. Just a few workers, mostly family."

"What kind of contracting?" Pop asked.

"Carpentry. Rough framing, some finishing work— for Negro customers, mostly, but they're doin' some jobs for white folks, too."

"Good for them. Always glad to hear about Negroes who own they own businesses."

"It's the future."

"Let's hope so."

Randall looked steadily at Pop. "When the war is over, after we're back, I'm gonna move to Atlanta and work for Sonny's family's company. I told him I'm a trained carpenter, and he says they'll be needin' good men, 'cause Atlanta is gonna grow real fast once soldiers come home and get jobs and start new families. Sonny checked with his dad, and he already wrote back with the job offer. I can start as soon as we get home."

"Move to *Atlanta?*" Ma asked.

The idea stunned me. Randall couldn't move away! I needed him. "Why didn't you tell me last night?" I asked.

He didn't seem to hear me. "Atlanta is my big chance, Ma. A chance to get ahead, make somethin' of my life. There ain't a thing for me here in Toad Hop. Or in Davisville, either."

"So yo' family don't count for anything—that what you sayin'?" Pop asked. "Our plans for you to come back and work with me, take over my puny little business one day when I'm too wore out to keep goin'? That ain't anything?"

"I don't mean it that way."

"How *do* you mean it?" Ma asked. "Your whole life is here—what little family you have is here. You don't know anyone in Atlanta."

"I know Sonny. He's got lots of friends my age. I'll get to know them, too. Up there, I can find a girl, get married, have a family. And get away from livin' like a slave in my own town."

"You think things are better up in Atlanta?" Pop asked.

"You still be stuck in the Deep South, least that's the last I heard."

"Sonny says things are better there. They got areas of town where it's almost all Negroes. You don't have to worry about white folks messin' with you all the time. God, Pop— I've had enough of white folks to last me my whole life!"

"You and me both, and I been havin' to put up with 'em a lot longer 'n you. But if you think you gonna get away from 'em by movin' up to Atlanta, you mistaken. White man rules the roost from here to Virginia and beyond. No gettin' around him."

I couldn't hold back any longer. "Don't leave," I pleaded. "What am I gonna do without you?"

Randall looked surprised. "I thought you'd want me to go, Caleb, as much as you hate it here, too. And here's an idea: you can come with me."

"Your brother ain't goin' nowhere!" Pop assured me. "You either. This is just one o' his big ideas. When the war is over, he gonna see things different."

Ma took out a handkerchief and began twisting it in her hands.

"No, I won't see things different, Pop! It's the war that's made me realize there's more to America than this dump, where men like Lee Davis lord it over everybody just because they got some money. I won't stay here—and I won't change my mind. You'll see."

"You gonna come back and work with me," Pop declared. "That what you promised me. I'm countin' on you."

"Let Caleb take my place."

"Hey, wait a minute—" I began.

Pop broke in. "Your brother ain't no more cut out to be a carpenter than you cut out to be the president. 'Sides, Caleb probably be rarin' to join you up in Atlanta. Leave his ma and me here to grow old and rot all by ourselves."

Randall was starting to lose his temper. "Pop, why do you have to be this way? Don't you want Caleb and me to have a better life?"

"Course I do. Your ma does, too. That's what all parents want for they children. But I can't see how runnin' off to Atlanta is gonna guarantee you that better life. You don't know this Sonny fella enough to trust anything he tell you. Hell, Randall! The world full of people with big ideas—people who make promises the way rabbits make babies."

"You never did trust me, Pop. That's what this is all about. You don't think I can make a good decision for myself. But I'm gonna do it. Just as soon as the war is over."

Ma stood up. "Let's please not argue this thing any more. I need Randall's visit to be a good one."

Pop got up and put his arms around Ma. "All right, sugar. All this is in the future. We can talk about it some other time."

"There ain't no reason to," Randall objected. "My mind's made up, and that's all there is to it."

Pop frowned at him but said nothing.

Ma went to her room, and Pop went to the porch to smoke his pipe. That left Randall and me to clean up. When we were done, Randall changed clothes, grabbed his wallet, and told me he'd be back later. He was headed for Tick's, the juke joint outside of Toad Hop, where he could get something to drink. And maybe Rose's after that.

I walked Randall out to the porch. I expected we'd run into Pop and that he and Randall would start wrangling again, but Pop wasn't there. Randall left, and I sat and watched the light fade down to gray, and then the stars came out, one by one. Still no Pop.

When the mosquitoes started biting, I went inside. Pop didn't come in, and there was no sign of Randall, so I finally went to bed.

A noise woke me up. Randall's bed was empty. I got up to see the time; the clock in the sitting room said two. There were voices on the porch—Pop's and Randall's. I moved toward the door and stood where it was dark and I couldn't be seen.

"I been waitin' for you," Pop was saying. "Why you out so late? You know what time it is?"

"I'm a grown man. Do I have to answer for everything I do?"

"Keep yo' voice down. I just want to know where you been. Down at Tick's, I reckon. You drunk, ain't you? That why you tripped on the steps."

I hoped they wouldn't start fighting again. It would upset Ma. If they got into it, I could go on the porch and try to stop them. I hoped it wouldn't happen.

"What if I am drunk?" Randall shot back at Pop. "It's my life."

"I told you to keep it down. Now we gonna talk."

"There's nothin' more to say."

"Oh, yes, they is! Sit down."

"Pop, I'm beat. Can't this keep till morning?"

"No, it can't keep till morning! I'm gonna knock this idea about goin' to Atlanta out of your head if it's the last thing I do."

"You can save your breath. I already told you: my mind's made up."

"I know you don't give a shit about me, but can't you stop and think about your ma? She already worried sick about losin' you in the war. Your comin' home safe will be her reward for all the prayers and sleepless nights she already been havin'. I don't like to think how much worse it gonna be once you ship out. You gonna break her heart by leavin' her again after you make it home?"

"Atlanta's not that far away. You and Ma will see me."

"I'm almost fifty years old, and I ain't never been to

Atlanta." Pop's voice sounded tight, like he was embarrassed to admit it. "What make you think things gonna change? You go up there, we might never see you again."

"Then I'll come see you. It ain't a big problem."

"Why you have to bring all this mess up now, on top of everything else we already got to handle?"

"Because I can't postpone actin' like a man in front of you anymore. Bein' in the army's changed me, Pop. I'd hoped you'd see that. My life is mine to live, whether you like it nor not. Guess I should have known you'd act this way."

"You ain't changed," Pop sneered. "Never a thought for anybody but yourself. That sums it all up, don't it? You and your brother just alike. It high time you both started thinkin'—about somethin' besides your own selves."

I could hear Randall get up. Now he'd go for Pop, and they'd tear each other apart. I started for the door. Then Randall said, "If Caleb and me are that bad, maybe you ought to think about how we got that way. We're your sons, Pop." He headed for the front door, and I hightailed it to our room and jumped into bed.

Randall came in a moment later and started to undress.

"Hey."

He turned around fast. "What are you doin' awake?"

"Listening to you and Pop fight."

"Oh, God! You heard all that mess?"

I told him yes. He lay down on top of his sheets.

"You mad at Pop?"

He sighed. "I dunno. More tired than mad. And sorry for Ma. Think what it's like for her, married to Pop all these years. And how do *you* stand it?"

"I stay out of his way. Like I told you: if he ever tries to lay a hand on me again, I'm gone."

"Good for you. The way Pop acted tonight—that makes me even more set on leaving. I'm serious about you comin' to Atlanta with me. As long as we live here, he'll try to run our lives. I'm sick of it."

"He thinks he knows best about everything, but he's wrong."

"Ah, hell! Let's not go over that ground again. There gotta be other things to talk about besides him." Randall paused for a moment. "Last night, you started to tell me somethin' about gettin' baptized. Least I think you did."

"Yeah, and you were so interested, you fell asleep."

"Sorry. Want to tell me now?"

I did, but how much should I tell? "I went ahead and did it for Ma's sake. She's been after me a long time."

"Just like she used to do me. Until she saw it was wasted breath."

"Pop's proud you see it his way."

"Oh, great! At least we see eye to eye on one thing. Did he try to stop you?"

"Naw, but when it was over, I got his speech about why he's against God and religion."

"He can't ever give that a rest! God, Caleb. We been hearin' that mess for years."

My heart was beating fast. This was my chance to share everything with my brother. I decided to tell him all about it. "Something . . . unusual happened when I got baptized."

"You get pond water up your nose?" Randall laughed at his joke.

"No, not that. Something crazy. Something I don't get."

"Yeah? Like what?"

It wasn't easy, because I knew what Randall thought, but I told him the whole story, including the only explanation that made any kind of sense: "The voice I told you about, that called my name and spoke to me right in this room—it was God."

"Oh, come on, Caleb! You don't really believe that."

I'd figured he'd be skeptical, but his reaction hurt anyway. "Yeah, I do. What else could it be?"

"Your imagination. A daydream. Your mind playin' tricks. Lots o' things."

"You're wrong. It was God."

"If God exists, he sure don't talk to people. You go around sayin' shit like that in the army, they label you a section eight and hustle you out of the service."

"Section eight?"

"A nut case. I've heard of guys tryin' stuff like that— 'God talked to me'—to try to get a discharge. The docs can usually tell the difference between the ones who are really off their rockers and the ones only pretending."

"I know what happened, and I'm not pretending."

"It was in your mind! Has it happened again since that day?"

"No—"

"You told anyone else?"

"I wanted to tell Ma, but she'd get all excited. You know how she is. And she'd probably tell Brother Johnson, make a big deal out of it."

"That's for sure. You best forget it."

"I can't!"

"Look, Caleb. It was just one of them strange things that happen—things we can't explain. Like how fortune-tellers are right sometimes."

There was no way to convince him. I'd tried, but he didn't get it.

"You always had the wildest imagination of anybody I know. Let it go." Randall said he was tired, turned over, and dropped into sleep.

"I know it was you," I told God. "How about letting me in on what you have in mind?"

God didn't, though, so there I was again, alone with my truth.

CHAPTER TEN

NATHAN KNOCKED at the window a little later. Randall was so dead to the world that he didn't even move when I climbed over him—watching where I put my feet—and went out.

At the creek, Nathan told me all about what had been going on at Lee Davis's place, where he was working in the fields. "I bet washin' dishes ain't nothin' compared to the excitement you been missin' at Old Man Davis's. It really been somethin' these past two days."

Nathan and his big talk. His imagination was a lot bigger than his brain. "Oh, sure. The excitement of chopping weeds. You can have it."

"It ain't what us Toad Hop folks been doin'. It's *other* folks and what *they* been doin' that make all the excitement. Just as good as a movie."

"Did a truckload of beautiful babes show up at Lee Davis's place for work?"

"I wish! Naw, we got ourselves twenty-five Germans!"

"Get out!"

"God's truth, my man! Mr. Lee didn't waste no time puttin' them in harness. They brought 'em over first thing yesterday morning and hustled 'em right into the fields. From the way they work, look like none of 'em is a farmboy. I guess in Germany they teach 'em how to use guns when they little, not hoes."

"They worked right there with you?"

"Naw. They kept 'em away from us, but not so far I couldn't see. Davis's man Stryker was there, showin' 'em what to do. They was soldiers with guns guardin' 'em, too."

I hated to admit it, but I was impressed. "Sounds pretty interesting. Were any of the Germans the guys we threw rocks at?"

Nathan shrugged. "I dunno. They was too far away to see 'em good."

"How'd it go?"

"Yesterday, smooth as silk. Today was different, though." He looked like a kid with a secret he was dying to tell but was going to make you beg to hear. Nathan could be annoying that way.

I had to play his game. "So tell me!"

Nathan looked so satisfied that I wanted to smack him. "All right. First off, couple o' prisoners try to make a break for it. I was mindin' my business, doin' my work, when I heard this shoutin', and looked up, and they was two of 'em, runnin' toward the woods at the back of the field." He acted out each happening as he went along, first working his hoe, then looking startled, and then becoming a prisoner, running away, arms pumping.

I had to smile. "Yeah? And then?"

"The guards shouted, and they just kept goin', and then they was gunshots, and that stop 'em! They fell down like they been hit, and for a second I thought maybe they been killed. Turn out the guards only fired into the air, and the men was smart enough to drop before another round come they way. Anyway, guards got 'em and marched 'em back to the truck. One of the guards hurries up to the big house while two others stand by the prisoners at the truck, they rifles ready."

"You're not making this up?" I asked Nathan.

He pretended to look hurt. "Cross my heart! Other guard be watchin' the rest o' the prisoners, yellin' at 'em to get back to work. Then here come the guard from the house, and after a while, Davis and Stryker come along, and then after that, another army truck come and take them two Nazis away in handcuffs and leg irons." Nathan folded his arms and looked at me like it was my turn to tell a good story. "Anything good as *that* happen at the Dixie Belle?"

Jealousy had me by the throat, but I had to be honest. "I can't top that."

He looked satisfied. "And that ain't all!"

"There's more?"

"Now don't you wish you was at Davis's with me, instead of slavin' in that kitchen? This afternoon, they was a fight. I couldn't see too good, since I was workin' at the other side o' the field, but I heard some noise again, and sure 'nough, some o' them Germans was goin' at each other. Two of 'em held this one guy while another one hit him in the face. Guards had to run in and break it up."

I didn't want to give Nathan the satisfaction of knowing it, but his story excited me and made me wish I could be part of it. "Anything else?" I asked coolly.

"Not much after that. The guards wasn't doin' nothin' before that 'cept standin' under the trees smokin', but now they had to stay right there in the field. The Germans went back to work, and that was that."

"What were they fighting about?"

"Who cares? Just keep 'em away from me. I don't want

nothin' to do with no Nazis. How's it goin' in the dish-washin' business?"

I told him about it, but it sounded dull compared to his adventure. Nathan spit when I mentioned Stewart Davis's name. And I told him some of Randall's stories about the army, and about Randall's fight with Pop.

By then, it felt really late, and we headed home. Randall didn't rouse when I climbed back over him. I was beat now, and it seemed like only a minute before Ma was waking me up for another day at the Dixie Belle.

* * *

After the breakfast rush was over, Mr. Davis and Miss Sondra came into the kitchen. She looked grim.

"Mornin', y'all," Mr. Davis said brightly. "How y'all doing today?"

"Makin' it," Aunt Lou replied. "Barely."

"That's why we're here. You know I always listen to you, Lou, just like I always have ever since I was young."

Aunt Lou just looked at him.

"My sister-in-law and I been discussing what you said about needing another helper, and we got the problem solved."

Miss Sondra's face was stony.

"Sondra don't think we can afford to hire anyone else for the kitchen. I disagree, the way the customers have been flockin' in here these past few days. But I always respect what the ladies have to say"—he smiled at Aunt Lou and Miss Sondra, who rolled her eyes, disgusted—"and so I figured out a way to give y'all some extra help."

I kept working away at my pans, wondering what Mr. Davis had up his sleeve.

"I got your new worker out in the dining room, and I'm gonna introduce y'all to him in a minute. They say he's a real good cook, too, since you need help in that department."

"Whatever you say, Mr. Lee," said Aunt Lou.

"So I want y'all to give him a chance. Everybody deserves a chance, don't they?"

"They shore do," Uncle Hiram agreed. "I been sayin' that all my life."

"I'll get him."

He went into the dining room and came back with our new helper. An MP came, too, because the new helper was a German prisoner.

Uncle Hiram put down the cheese grater and stared. Aunt Lou stayed in her chair, and she stared, too.

The prisoner was wearing blue trousers and a white T-shirt, and he held a blue cap. He was young, maybe Randall's age. Thin, and his hair, the color of cornsilk, was cut short. A red birthmark the size of a pecan on his right cheek. And a swollen, purple left eye. He'd been in a fight.

"Who that?" Aunt Lou put down her pipe. "I ain't never seen him before."

"Course not," Mr. Davis said cheerfully. "He ain't from around here. Fact is, this boy come all the way across the Atlantic Ocean just to work in your kitchen, Lou."

"One of them prisoners from that new camp?"

"Yes, ma'am! This here's Andreas. He's a trained chef, according to Colonel Ross, the fellow that runs Camp Davis. Ross says he's a good fella, quiet, hard worker. He won't give you any trouble."

I felt like laughing at Mr. Davis's nerve. Only a man as rich and powerful as he was could get away with a scheme like this. But glancing at the prisoner, I felt a little shaky, too. He looked harmless enough, but he was an enemy, after all.

Aunt Lou pushed herself out of her chair and confronted Mr. Davis. "You gon' bring one o' *them* into my kitchen? Them that's fightin' against our boys, killin' 'em? That how you gon' 'help us out'?"

"Andreas here is gonna be a *big* help. He promised Ross he would. Y'all don't need to worry about a thing," Mr. Davis went on. "The guard'll stay around for a couple days if you want him to, until y'all feel comfortable. But I promise that nothin' is gonna happen. Andreas ain't got nowhere to go and no one to help him. If he gives you a lick o' trouble, he'll end up in the stockade, and he don't want that."

"Thank you, Mr. Lee," Uncle Hiram declared. "Everything gon' work out good. Don't you worry none. Lou and me can take care o' things."

"I know y'all will. Just put him to work. If he gives you trouble, let the guard know." He patted the prisoner on the back. "You do what they tell you, hear? They'll take good care of you, long as you mind your manners."

The prisoner—Andreas—didn't say anything.

"Let's let these folks get acquainted," Mr. Davis told Miss Sondra. "See y'all later!" He went toward the door, then turned back. "Oh, one thing I forgot to tell y'all. Andreas don't speak any English."

"No English?" Aunt Lou cried, getting right up in Andreas's face.

He understood her. *"Nein,"* he replied, shaking his head like he was all sorry.

"How'm I gon' talk to you, then? Answer me that!"

He shrugged and looked pitiful.

Much as I disliked Mr. Lee Davis, I had to hand it to him. He was a slippery customer. Aunt Lou had wanted an extra helper, and now she had one. Even if he could really cook, which remained to be seen, he was an enemy soldier who couldn't speak her language. But Mr. Davis had produced that extra pair of hands—cheap.

Aunt Lou kept looking at Andreas like she'd never seen a blond-headed white boy before. Then she began to untie her apron. "I'm done!" she cried. "Enough is enough."

Uncle Hiram came to the rescue again. "No need to get all outdone, sugar. You leave this boy to me. I can put him to work. It be all right." He looked at the guard. "We got this under control, sir. You can go set in the dining room if you want. We can bring you a cup o' coffee and some cake in a minute."

The guard didn't say no.

Aunt Lou squirmed away from Uncle Hiram's arms. "Y'all might as well carry me over to Milledgeville right now, so I can finish goin' crazy. Ain't we fighting a war 'gainst them Germans? We might as well give this one the butcher knife and let him cut our throats."

Aunt Lou had a point, despite her dramatics.

"We got dinner to finish," Uncle Hiram reminded us all. "Lou, you and me can talk this over later."

All this time, Andreas just stood there, messing with his cap. He didn't need to know a word of English to understand what was going on.

"Come on, young fella," Uncle Hiram said. "Might as well make the best of it. I's Uncle Hiram." He laid one hand on his chest. "Can you say that?"

"Hiram."

"Good! And this here is Aunt Lou."

"*Tante* Lou."

"How's that?"

"*Tante.*"

"What's he mean?"

"How in hell should I know?" Aunt Lou shot back.

I thought I knew. "Maybe that's German for 'aunt.'"

"Shore! That's it! Thanks, Caleb. You one smart boy." He addressed Andreas again, pointing at me. "And this here is Caleb."

"We can't stand here passin' the time," Aunt Lou said. "I got chicken to fry and cornbread to bake."

"And I got meat loaf to mix up," Uncle Hiram remembered. "Caleb, you and Andreas get them taters peeled. Then y'all can do the fruit salad. I'll fetch that guard his cake an' coffee."

Handing Andreas the sharp paring knife felt strange after what Aunt Lou had said. I told myself it was stupid to worry.

Right away, it was clear he knew what he was doing. For every potato I peeled, he did two or three. I found myself watching him and trying to figure out how he worked so fast. We got done in no time, then went on to the fruit salad. After that, we cut cucumbers and onions for a vinegar salad, and then we sliced up the chocolate sheet cakes and put the pieces on plates. Having someone to help made it all easier—fun, almost.

As we worked, Andreas looked around. He watched

how Aunt Lou could do three things at once and nodded like he appreciated her efficiency. He studied the food—the butter beans, black-eyed peas with ham hocks, the dressing made from yesterday's leftover biscuits, the yellow squash casserole. Aunt Lou made a point of ignoring him, but she had to notice how much he wanted to help and how interested he seemed.

English or no English, Andreas made a difference, even that first morning, and when Miss Sondra came in to announce that the first dinner customers had arrived, we were ready.

When the rush was over, Aunt Lou told me to take Andreas into the alley, where she brought us two heaping plates of food. Andreas tasted everything. He wolfed down the pork chop and fried chicken legs, the mashed potatoes and gravy, too, and some of the black-eyed peas and mustard greens. He wouldn't eat the squash casserole. Uncle Hiram brought us some cake, and Andreas cleaned his plate. I watched him eat and wondered how long it had been since he'd had food as good as Aunt Lou's.

When we were done, Andreas brought out a pack of Camels and offered me one. I took it and we lit up. I wanted to talk to him, ask him a lot of questions. Where in Germany was his home? How did he get into the army? Had he been in battle, killed anyone? What did he think about America? And then there was that swollen eye. Was he the prisoner Nathan had seen get beat up? He seemed friendly enough, and he was a hard worker, but that didn't make up for one thing: Andreas was a German soldier, captured because he was fighting against America. Against soldiers like Randall. Still, here I was, eating dinner with him and smoking one of his cigarettes.

CHAPTER ELEVEN

THE NEXT EVENING we were sitting on the porch when Lee Davis drove up in his shiny black LaSalle.

"What the hell do he want?" Pop muttered. "He ain't come out here to pass the time o' day."

Mr. Davis hoisted himself out of the driver's seat and came to the porch. We all got to our feet. "How you doin', Mr. Lee?" Pop asked. "Come on the porch and set a while. Lucy be glad to get you a cold drink."

"Thanks, Frank, but not now. I can't stay away from home too long. Mama's not doing well. She's gone senile, if you want to know the truth. I wouldn't tell just anyone, but we've been friends a long time, and I know y'all care about Mama. She gets right fretful sometimes if I'm not around."

We all said how sorry we were to hear all that and prayed that Miss Evelyn would soon be feeling better.

"I appreciate that," Mr. Davis replied, "but I don't believe she *can* get better. Only a miracle could do anything for Mama now." Then he pulled himself together. "I just wanted to come by and say hey to our soldier boy and let him know how proud we all are that one of our own is fightin' the good fight of freedom."

"Thanks, Mr. Lee," Randall said. "You're right thoughtful to come by to tell me that." Mr. Davis would never guess that Randall despised him—or that Pop did, too.

"One more thing. I've arranged somethin' good for y'all. I just cut a deal with the state to bring electric lines out this way. Toad Hop is gonna have power at last."

For once, Pop looked genuinely pleased. "That's mighty good news, Mr. Lee. Mighty good. We been waitin' a long time for that."

Davis looked pleased, too. "What are you gonna get first, Lucy?"

"Well, sir, I'd like a light in each room. Not having to use lanterns and candles anymore will be real nice. And then I'd like to have an electric iron instead of having to heat flatirons on the stove."

"You, Frank?"

"A radio."

"Sure! You want to listen to that comedy show about colored folks—*Amos 'n' Andy*."

"Yes, sir," Pop said, careful always to agree. "But I want to be able to follow the news, too. I'm mighty interested to know how the war is goin'."

The white man's smile faded a bit. He didn't like it when Negroes acted interested in government or politics or world events. But Mr. Davis remembered his manners and put his smile back in place. "Of course you do, Frank. What with Randall about to go over there, y'all want to hear the news. Guess who I got to put up the poles for the power lines? The prisoners! I told Colonel Ross there wasn't much farm work to do just now, it being so early in the growing season, and I suggested we could keep some of his boys busy. He agreed right away. Soon as the supplies get here, we're good to start. Toad Hop's gonna have electricity before you know it!"

We all repeated how thankful we were, and Mr. Davis said it was time to get going. He wished Randall lots of luck and told him to go over there and kick some Germans' backsides and then come home safe. Naturally he didn't offer to shake hands.

At the car he remembered something else. "By the way, Frank, Caleb's doin' real good at the Dixie Belle. We're happy you could spare him this summer."

"Glad it worked out." Pop sure didn't sound glad.

"Caleb tell you about our new kitchen helper?"

"No, sir."

"Aunt Lou kept fussin' about needin' more hands—y'all know how *she* is—so I arranged for one of them prisoners to work at the restaurant. The fellow is a trained cook, too! Strange world, ain't it? Here we are, fightin' this war, and our boys are goin' overseas to take care of business, and fellows from the other side end up here in Davisville! Might as well squeeze some work out of 'em long as they're here."

With that, he got in the car, waved at us, and drove away.

Randall spoke first. "Cracker comes out here to tell us he's doin' us a favor, and all I want to do is punch him."

"Mr. Davis didn't *have* to get them to bring electricity out here," I pointed out.

Randall looked disgusted. "Jeez, Caleb! When he ain't around, plain ol' 'Davis' is good enough for him."

"*More* than he deserve," Pop added. "I'll allow he done us a favor, but some so-called favors ain't worth the cost."

I waited. Pop was working himself up to say something ugly.

He turned to me. "So, how's it feel to be rubbin' shoulders with somebody who'd just as soon kill your brother as look at him? It warn't enough to go runnin' to the white man for a job. Only you could of found a place where you got to breathe the same air as one of them Nazis."

"That ain't fair!" Randall exclaimed.

Pop ignored him. "You get to listen while that Hun talk about all the fun he had shootin' Allied soldiers?"

I could answer this. "We don't talk about anything. He can't speak English."

"Course not! If Hitler has his way, all of us be speakin' *German* before it's over. I bet your new friend know how to pull a trigger and use a bayonet, though."

"It ain't Caleb's fault," Randall said. "Lay off him, Pop."

"Don't you tell me what to do! This is between Caleb and me, so you can shut up."

"Frank, please!" Ma said.

Randall stepped between Pop and me. "I don't mean to disrespect you, but it ain't Caleb's fault that Lee Davis'll do anything to save himself a buck—even deal with our enemies. And don't forget: Caleb ain't the only one got to be around 'em. Anybody from Toad Hop workin' for Davis this summer is gonna have to do the same. You don't blame *them*."

"They ain't workin' for Davis to spite they own father. Caleb had him a decent job, but he warn't satisfied with that." Pop shook his head at me. "I hope you real pleased with yourself. You wanted to spend your summer with the white folks, and now you got your wish. And you got yourself a Nazi, too."

"Oh, Pop, quit it," Randall exclaimed. "We all know how you feel about it. Why can't you let it go? Just forgive him."

"So now you preachin' at me!"

"No, sir. Just tellin' you the truth. Tellin' you what Ma and the rest of us are thinking."

"I see. Now you know what everybody be thinkin'. They must teach a bunch o' stuff in the army they didn't teach back in my day. Like how to read minds."

Ma touched Pop's arm. "Let's not fight. Mr. Lee came out here with *good* news. Just think, Frank. A radio! And an iron. And electric lights in every room. No more kerosene lanterns!"

"I hope Davis can deliver the goods. Be nice if *somethin'* good come out o' all this mess."

I had to agree.

* * *

Maybe Ma talked some sense into Pop that night, because he didn't go on grousing about me working at the Dixie Belle with Andreas. For his part, Andreas was the same the next day, and the next. He did what he was told and looked for more work, too. When I watched him peeling potatoes, mopping the floor, or enjoying a plate of food next to me in the back alley, I couldn't imagine him wanting to kill Randall or any American soldier, or even firing a rifle. I tried to imagine him a Nazi, a cold-blooded killer, but I couldn't.

I reckoned I should hate him, but I couldn't do that either. After all, he hadn't done anything to me. I prayed about it. When I opened Grandpa's Bible one afternoon, I came to the place where Jesus said we're supposed to love God with all our hearts and souls and minds—and our neighbors as ourselves. In one way Andreas wasn't a neighbor, but in another way he kind of was.

Betty Jean seemed to be reading from that same page, because she was nice to Andreas. Not Voncille. She hated his guts. I heard Betty Jean tell Voncille she thought Andreas was handsome, and Voncille let her have it.

"I can't believe what I'm hearin'!" she cried. "You're an American, ain't you?"

"Yes, ma'am."

"And he's a German! One of Hitler's killers. They've overrun most of Europe! And you know what they do when they take over a place."

"No, ma'am."

Voncille must have whispered something, then she said, "That's right. Women, young girls—girls like you. And you stand there and tell me you think he's good-lookin'? Wake up, Betty Jean! If he makes one move toward you . . . I wish he'd give *me* a reason to fix him. Just bein' in the same room with him makes me sick."

"Why do you stay here, then?" Betty Jean wanted to know.

"'Cause jobs are hard to come by! And when the war is over and they ship this Andreas and all the rest of 'em back where they belong, I hope to still be working here. The tips ain't bad, when you come right down to it. Understand?"

"Yes, ma'am."

"All right, then. So don't let me hear you say another word about him. There's only one thing he wants from you, and he'd be happy to kill you after he got it."

Andreas, a killer? A rapist?

* * *

Randall's leave was going by fast, and I wasn't seeing him much. The Dixie Belle took my days, and Randall went to Tick's after supper to keep out of Pop's way. Two nights before his leave ended, I reminded Randall what we'd agreed on, and when we were sure the folks were asleep, out the window we went.

"So what do you want to do?" Randall asked me. "This is your night."

I couldn't think of much; just being with my brother was enough. "We could go swimming."

"And freeze our asses off, this early in the spring. But if you want to, I'm game. What else?"

"Could we get something to drink?"

"A Coke? Sure thing."

"Not that. Something . . . stronger."

"You mean liquor? You tryin' to get Pop to kill me? 'Cause if he finds out, that's just what he'll do."

"He won't find out, not if we're careful."

"Now you sound like me. What happened to that scared little brother I used to know?"

"How about some cigarettes?"

"Jeez, Caleb. Why not? And I got another idea, too."

Randall led the way around the back of Toad Hop and out into the country, toward Tick's. As we approached, I could hear jazzy music and the sounds of people talking and laughing.

"You stay here. This won't take long."

When Randall came back, he had a brown paper sack. "I got us some good stuff. Real smooth. You'll like it."

"Great. Let's go to the pond. Nobody'll be around."

"Not yet. We got something else to take care of first." With that, he started off again.

"Where we going?"

"Rose's."

My heart started to pound. "For real?"

"It's your time. You want to drink, smoke—just like I was doin' by the time I was your age. Only one thing left. Time you had yourself a woman. How about it?"

"I guess so." I wasn't really sure, but I couldn't let Randall know that. "All right."

"That's it! Nothin' to be nervous about. Rose'll treat you good."

I really wanted to turn around and head back to Toad Hop. But I wanted this other thing, too.

We came to the back of Rose's place. Light shone through the curtained windows of her cabin. I was sweating.

"Come on. She's home. I'll introduce you."

I followed him through the shadows of the tall pines. It was so dark I couldn't see much, and that's why I bumped into Randall when he came to a sudden stop.

"Goddamn it," he muttered.

"What?"

"Look for yourself."

Stewart Davis's red roadster was parked in front of Rose's place.

"Come on! We don't want nothing here. Not now."

"Wait a second." I pushed past him so I could get a better view of the yard. It was quiet, nobody in sight. I took my clasp knife out, flipped open the blade, and hurried over to the car. The blade pierced the right front tire like a hot knife through butter. It did the back tire just as good. In a few seconds, I was back with Randall, and now I was the one pulling him into the woods and safety.

He didn't speak until we were far away from Rose's place. Then he stopped and faced me. "God, Caleb! Why'd you do that?"

I felt like telling the world. "He had it coming!"

"I been into some crazy stuff in my day, but you just beat the hell out of anything I *ever* done. Do you know what'll happen if he finds out who cut his tires?"

I had impressed my big brother, the soldier. "He won't find out. He won't tell anyone, if he can help it."

"You're right about that. I wish we could be there when he finds he got *two* bad tires! Look like he's gonna have a long walk home and a lot of explainin' to do when he gets there."

I enjoyed imagining how Stewart would try to get himself out of the mess I'd made for him.

Back in Toad Hop, we sat on the dock at Hale's Pond. The bourbon was good, a lot smoother than Mr. Artie's nasty moonshine. We were quiet, sipping from the bottle, smoking our Lucky Strikes, and watching for shooting stars, like we used to do when we were kids.

"Let's have that swim," Randall suggested. He stood up and started to undress. In a moment, he was in his drawers. "What you waiting for?"

I got to my feet, and for a second I felt lightheaded.

"Steady. Take a deep breath."

My head cleared, and I stripped to my drawers, too.

"Ready?"

I wasn't sure. The night air felt cool and the pond water was inky black.

"Watch out!" Randall shoved me and I hit the water hard. My head went under, and for a moment I couldn't figure which way was up. But I came to the surface, shivering. And there was Randall on the dock, laughing. "How's the water?"

"You danged fool! That wasn't funny."

"Yeah, it was. Nothing like some cold water to sober you up."

"I'm not drunk!"

"Just tipsy." Then he jumped in. "Man alive, it *is* cold! Ooowee!"

"Told you."

He swam to me and grabbed me around the chest. "Let's see how strong you got since I been gone."

I fought back, trying to get away, but his arms were like iron. Nothing worked until I remembered to tickle him. He always hated that.

"Hey! No fair."

I broke away and tried to swim, but he caught my leg and started to pull me back. So I went for him. We wrestled and fooled around like we were kids again. Randall dunked me good a couple times, and I splashed water in his face, which he hated, and we wrestled some more.

Then we floated on our backs and rested. The water didn't feel cold now; it felt great. Above us, the stars were bright.

"Let's dry off," Randall suggested. The air felt chilly on my skin, and I wished I had a towel. Randall drank again and offered me more, but I'd had enough.

"I got somethin' to say to you," Randall told me after another Lucky Strike. "If anything happens to me—"

"Don't!"

"Just listen, okay? If somethin' happens to me, Pop and Ma are gonna need you."

"To do what?"

Randall lighted a match and watched it burn. "To be the kind of son they always wanted."

"*You're* the son they want, not me. Pop's proud of you."

"You think so? After I run off and enlisted?"

"You'd have been drafted anyway."

"I know, but I was desperate to get away. Away from Pop. All we ever done is fight."

"And now he won't leave me alone."

"Since I been gone, I've figured somethin' out. Pop *needs* someone to fight, but it ain't really you or me he's mad at. It's white folks, but they're too strong for him. So he takes it out on us."

"It's not fair!"

"Don't I know it! Wish I had the answer. But Pop's been mad at the world his whole life."

"How long's he gonna hold it against me for working at the Dixie Belle?"

"Who knows? Don't take this the wrong way, Caleb, but I'm kinda glad he picks on you instead of Ma. She puts up with enough even without that."

"I don't know what to do."

"You could quit the restaurant and come back and work with him. That might help."

"And let him win? Uh-uh!"

Randall put his hand on my shoulder. "Pop needs you."

"Like hell! He doesn't need anyone unless it's someone to bully."

"That ain't true and you know it. If somethin' happens to me, he'll need you and Ma real bad."

I turned away. "Stop talking that way! Nothing is gonna happen to you. It can't."

"I used to think that, too. But then they had us write our wills in camp. Somehow, that made it real. Look at me, Caleb."

I turned around and faced him.

"I could be killed, and we got to accept it. It's hard for the folks to think about it, so you're the lucky one."

"Gee, thanks."

"Sorry, man. But I'm glad I got you to hear me out."

That made me feel good, even though I hated this conversation.

"So think about coming back and working with Pop."

"Maybe, if he starts treating me right."

Randall touched my shoulder again. "Promise me you'll think about it."

"All right."

"Fair enough. You want some more to drink?"

Now I did, and we passed the bottle.

"Get up," Randall told me.

We faced each other, and he put his arms around me. I held on to him, and we didn't speak, because no words were enough.

Randall let me go. "Put 'em up!" Before I could move, he slapped me lightly on the cheek. "Lemme see if you'll turn the other one." He laughed, and I did, too, and then we boxed. He landed a couple good ones on me, and I got him on the chest.

When we'd had enough, both of us panting, Randall threw his arm over my shoulder. "I love you, Caleb, and I know I can count on you, no matter what."

Of all the things Randall had ever said to me, that was the best.

CHAPTER TWELVE

WE WERE UP early the morning Randall had to leave. Ma was silent as she served breakfast. Afterward, Randall went to our room to get his duffle bag. I followed him and sat on my bed, trying to think of something to say, but my mind was empty.

Ma came to the door. "All packed?"

"Yes, ma'am."

She looked at the list in her hand. "Razor and shaving soap?"

"Uh-huh."

"Clean underwear, socks, toothbrush and toothpaste, sewing kit, foot powder . . ."

Randall laughed. "You checked it all yesterday!"

"Oh, I bought you some stationery. And some choco-late bars and chewing gum, too."

"You thought of everything."

"That's a mother's job." Ma wiped away tears.

Randall went to her. "Don't. Please don't cry, Ma."

"Promise me you'll be careful! Don't take any chances. No one needs you to be a hero, but we need you to come home."

"I will. War's gonna be over soon—before you know it."

"I'll be praying for you. Every day, Psalm Ninety-One: 'A thousand may fall at thy side, ten thousand at thy right hand, but it shall not come near thee.'"

"Thanks, Ma."

"And you pray, too. Promise me!"

From the yard, Pop started calling for us to come on or Randall would miss his train.

Ma hurried away to get her hat and her purse. Randall took one last look around our room, squeezed my shoulder, and grabbed his stuff. "Don't *you* look so glum," he told me. "I can't stand that. Remember what I told you."

"I will."

"Heck, Caleb! This ain't the end of the world. It's the start of my biggest adventure."

* * *

At the station we waited in silence. Then the train came along and Randall found the Colored Only car. He hugged Ma, shook hands with Pop, and hugged me, too. I could feel tears coming, but I held them back. Pop put his arm around Ma, and he looked pretty rough himself. Randall got on, found a seat by the window, and waved to us until the train disappeared.

"Let's go home," Pop told Ma. I headed to the Dixie Belle, feeling lower than I had since the evening Pop whipped me.

The place was hopping, as usual, which was good—it kept me too busy to be sad. After we cleaned up, Aunt Lou cleared a space on the worktable, and Andreas brought out a big bowl, measuring cups, and some spoons.

"Andreas is gon' bake us some German bread," Uncle Hiram told me. "Seem he say somethin' at the camp about wantin' to do it, and they bring Lou word, askin' if it be all right. This mornin', they sent over some special German stuff from the camp, from what they ordered for the prisoners to eat. Andreas want to show us what his folks eat over in Germany."

Aunt Lou looked up from the stew she was simmering. "Miz Sondra say if he can cook good, we might could put some o' his stuff on the menu. We see about that."

In between doing his regular chores to help get dinner ready, Andreas mixed up his bread dough, kneaded it, and let it rise. By the time we were done with the dinner rush, he had two loaves of warm rye bread ready for us to eat. It smelled delicious, the way fresh-baked bread always does. I'd never eaten that kind of bread, and I wasn't sure I'd like it, but it tasted as good as it smelled. We all had some, even Betty Jean and Miss Sondra. Not Voncille, though. She left the minute dinner was over.

Andreas looked pleased that everyone liked his bread.

"Ist gut, ja?" he said. "I make again? Maybe tomorrow?"

"Well, I be!" Aunt Lou cried. "You mean to say you can talk English? You been understandin' everything we been sayin' all this time?"

He shook his head. *"Nein.* English—no, not so good. *Nur ein bisschen*—just a little."

"From now on, y'all better watch what you say," Miss Sondra warned.

"I make tomorrow?" Andreas repeated. *"Das Brot?"*

She looked at him coolly. "I don't see why not. As long as you can do all your other work first. Maybe we can order some Swiss cheese. Some of our customers don't want a full meal at dinner, and perhaps they'd enjoy a Swiss on rye. With a dill pickle on the side. We'll see."

After she left, Aunt Lou said that woman would put chicken-fried rattlesnake on her menu if she thought she could make an extra buck.

At home Ma was taking down laundry. Everything on the line was Randall's—sheets, towels, clothes he'd worn while he was on leave. "I'll have a lot of ironing tomorrow," she said. "Something to keep me busy."

In our room Randall's bed was remade with fresh sheets, his dresser dusted, and all of his things put away. Seeing it all so neat made me feel strange. Randall might never be coming back to sleep here. He'd come home from the war and go off to Atlanta.

We ate a quiet supper, and Pop helped me wash dishes, a chore he hated. I could tell he was trying to be extra nice for Ma's sake.

Two days later we had a letter from Randall, letting us know he'd gotten to Fort Gordon okay. They were going to have some extra training and be issued their gear for overseas. Soon he'd be on his way to Norfolk, and then Europe.

* * *

I was walking to work on a Tuesday morning in June— June 6, 1944, to be exact. The sound of a wagon coming fast toward Toad Hop got me off the road. It was Isaac Washington, who worked a night shift cleaning offices in Davisville. He stopped when he saw me.

"Mornin', Caleb. Your daddy up yet?"

"Not when I left. What's your hurry, Mr. Isaac? Anything wrong?"

"Big news. Wonderful news! I was cleanin' up the newspaper office just now when word come over the wire. They give me a copy to share with folks." He pulled a crumpled paper from his pocket. "Here."

I knew Mr. Isaac couldn't read, so I read it out loud. "'Under the command of General Eisenhower, Allied naval forces supported by strong air forces began landing Allied armies this morning on the northern coast of France.' What's it mean?"

"The invasion of Europe done started, that what! Hitler been pushin' 'gainst the rest of Europe long enough, and we gon' push back. Mr. Sam say he bet we be in Berlin by July."

"Will Randall still have to go?"

"Can't say. I pray not. Well, let me get on, now. Your daddy's gon' want to know, and then we can spread the word. Wouldn't be surprised if Brother Cecil call a service of thanksgiving for this evenin'."

He urged the horse on, and I went on my way. My mind kept coming back to Ma. For her sake, I hoped Randall wouldn't have to go. Maybe the men at the newspaper office were right—maybe the war would end real soon and Randall could stay in America, where he belonged.

At the Dixie Belle they'd already heard the news. I hadn't seen Aunt Lou look so happy since I'd started working there. She hugged me and said that for sure Randall would be coming home now.

"We pray so," Uncle Hiram added, "but the radio say it a long way from France over to Germany, and they's a lot o' German soldiers between our boys and Berlin. And don't forget about them Japs."

"No more o' that," Aunt Lou scolded him. "This ain't no mornin' to be spreadin' no gloom. Mr. Roosevelt and Mr. Churchill been sayin' all along we gon' win this war, and we *are* gon' win it! Only a matter o' time now."

"You right, honey. All I'm sayin' is, it ain't gon' be no easy road."

"Bless God Randall ain't in it," Aunt Lou told me. "I pray the Lord Jesus protect every one o' our boys this day."

That's when Andreas came through the back door.

"Good morning," he said. How could he not notice we were all staring at him? "Is good day. America— Eisenhower—fight. Is good."

"Good?" Uncle Hiram exclaimed. "It *bad* news for y'all, ain't it?"

"America fight Germany." His words came out slowly. "Win Germany. Is good." He went to the closet to get his apron.

"If that don't beat all," Uncle Hiram said. "That boy want *us* to win? Why'd he fight for them Nazis, then?"

"Probably didn't have no choice," Aunt Lou replied. "Probably got hisself drafted the way most o' our boys did."

Andreas came back in and set to work in silence. He kept to himself, working like a machine. Voncille came in, gave him a smug look, and made a big point of telling us all how happy she was and what a great day had come at last. I hoped Andreas's English was as bad as he claimed, because he didn't need to hear all that. For all we knew, he had a brother or someone in the fighting.

That was a busy morning. Lots of folks came to eat, celebrating the first good news we'd had in a while. They played "Don't Sit Under the Apple Tree" and "The White Cliffs of Dover" on the jukebox. Even Miss Sondra was in a good mood.

Through it all, Andreas kept his face set. What was in his mind? I glanced at him peeling potatoes for dinner and couldn't imagine hearing that the Germans had invaded America and feeling glad about it. How could Andreas want his country to lose this war?

For two days Ma held on to the hope that D-day meant Randall's orders to Europe would be canceled. But the Germans were fighting for every foot of ground. Although our troops managed to land at Normandy and capture some towns, thousands of men were dying. The road to Berlin would be one big battle.

All our hopes that Randall could stay in the States

ended with his letter saying his unit was heading for Norfolk and then Europe. Some lines had been marked out with black ink, and Pop said the censors had gotten to it.

Then we didn't hear from Randall for a couple weeks. We'd heard about German U-boats sinking our ships right off the coast of North Carolina, so it was a relief when we got a letter from Naples, Italy, telling us Randall had arrived safe and sound.

Every day Ma's face looked a little older. Every day Pop looked more worried. He stopped giving me such a hard time, though. I guess he realized how it upset Ma when he picked on me. Every day I had to work with Andreas, knowing that his country had started all this trouble. And almost every day I had to watch Stewart Davis come into the kitchen, get in the way, help himself to everything, and act like the place belonged to him. If his daddy scolded him, it hadn't done any good. It wasn't fair that a draft dodger like him was here at home while decent, brave guys like Randall were off trying to drive the Nazis out of their conquered territories. Thoughts like that made me want to slash some more tires.

For a while I waited for God to talk to me again, but he didn't. Maybe Randall had been right, I sometimes thought. Maybe it was just my imagination. But later I'd change my mind again. It *had* happened; it *was* God. But the longer God kept quiet, the easier it was to forget about him. One day I realized I hadn't thought about him in a week. That embarrassed me. From then on I prayed to him every night, but it wasn't to ask him to speak to me again. I prayed for Randall to come home safe.

CHAPTER THIRTEEN

LEE DAVIS GOT HIS WAY, and soon work started on bringing electricity to Toad Hop. I saw it happen because I walked to town every day. The prisoners began putting the poles in the ground. Later, men from the power company would come and string the wires.

One evening not long after the work had begun, we were sitting on the front porch, trying to stay cool. The weather was unusually hot for June, and Ma was fanning herself. Miss Suzy Jackson, the "Church Mother" of Holy Zion congregation, appeared in the yard and Ma invited her to come up and sit a spell.

I figured something was up. Miss Suzy took her role

in the church very seriously. Pop said one day she'd get rid of Brother Johnson and take over the preaching herself. Ma told Pop that wasn't funny, but she allowed that Miss Suzy could be overbearing. Still, she meant well. But I agreed with Pop. If you didn't get out of Miss Suzy's way, she'd run right over you. And she was big enough to do it, too.

Miss Suzy accepted Ma's offer of pound cake and coffee and got right down to business. "Some o' us ladies met this afternoon and decided we wants to do somethin' nice for them men what's workin' so hard to bring the power out our way."

"Like what?" Ma asked.

"You know what the Lord say 'bout how we suppose to feed the hungry and give drink to the thirsty and visit them what's in prison. Not only that: we all suppose to follow the golden rule."

"Certainly—"

"Well, so far, ain't no one done a blessed thing for them German mens! They in prison, ain't they, and who 'mong us has paid them one visit? That mean we disobeyin' God's holy word."

"I don't know about God's holy word," Pop put in, "but ain't no one gonna be allowed inside that camp to visit. And as for them bein' hungry and thirsty, from what I hear, Uncle Sam takin' plenty good care of 'em. Word is, they eat better than some folks right here in Toad Hop! And got better roofs over they heads, too."

"I didn't say they goin' hungry," Miss Suzy replied evenly. "But they ain't nothin' keepin' us from showin' 'em a little kindness. After all, they doin' us a big favor."

"Like they got a choice in the matter! Davis sniffed out a way to get some free labor, and somebody signed a paper okayin' the deal, and them prisoners didn't have one word to say about it one way or 'nother. You think them Huns give a damn 'bout whether we get power or not? Nazis got about as much use for Negroes as they got for Jews. If they had they way, we'd all be dead."

"Lucy," Miss Suzy went on, ignoring Pop, "you ain't never been one to go against the Word of the Lord. Why, everyone in the church look up to you as a model of Christian charity!"

Ma glanced at Pop like she was hoping he'd get her off the hook somehow, but he didn't say anything. "What are the ladies thinking of doing?"

Miss Suzy brightened. "We thought it be right nice to bake up some sweet cakes, cookies, and such. Cold lemonade, too. After dinner sometime soon, carry everything over to where they workin'. They'd like that."

"I suppose," Ma replied, without enthusiasm.

"We thought you could bake up a couple o' your pound cakes. No one make pound cake good as you, child." To prove her point, Miss Suzy took a huge bite and sighed with happiness. "We thought to do it day after tomorrow. That give everyone time to buy they ingredients and do they baking. And that remind me: my sugar ration stamps is all used up. You got any left?"

"I believe so."

"Don't suppose you could share any?" This wasn't the first time Miss Suzy had come begging for some of Ma's ration stamps. "I ain't askin' for myself. This is for a good cause. Sometimes we got to sacrifice if we intend to obey the Lord," she added grandly.

The expression on Pop's face made me want to laugh.

"Let me see what I have." Ma found her ration book. "Yes, I have some sugar stamps left."

Miss Suzy almost grabbed them. "Tell you what, Lucy. Since you been good enough to sacrifice these for a act of Christian mercy, I'll go to town for you—save you a trip. Is they anything else you need?"

"Ain't no guarantee you gonna find sugar," Pop cautioned. "Just 'cause you got you some stamps don't mean Mr. Ellison gonna have sugar."

"We just got to have faith he will. 'Where the Lord guide, he provide.'"

"See if he has any vanilla," Ma said. "Here's some money."

"And will you come with us when we go? Brother Ford is gon' let us use his wagon."

"I don't know—"

"We *need* you, child! Couldn't make it without you. That's settled, then. Now please tell me what y'all hear from Randall. You know what a favorite he is with me."

"May I be excused?" I asked. I didn't want to hear Miss Suzy gush about Randall or pump Ma for news about stuff that wasn't her business.

"Oh, Caleb. How you be? I didn't hardly notice you sittin' over there so quiet. How you enjoy workin' at the Dixie Belle? And what about that prisoner they got there?"

I glanced at Pop, wondering if he'd react. He didn't, and I felt grateful. "It's all right," I assured her. "Pop, I need to go over to Nathan's. We're going fishing."

He said I could, and I guessed he wished he could come with me.

* * *

Next day Miss Suzy brought what Ma needed, and Ma baked her pound cakes, like she promised. The day after that the ladies of Toad Hop surprised the prisoners with what Pop insisted on calling their "little afternoon tea party."

Ma told us about it over supper. "The prisoners weren't at all what I expected."

"Oh?" Pop didn't sound interested.

"Until today, I hadn't even seen one of them. Why would I? And now that I have, I don't know what to think. They were friendly, Frank. Respectful—and so grateful."

"What you expect? You give a hungry man a piece o' your pound cake, course he gonna be grateful."

"That's sweet. By the way, I saved some for you and Caleb. You can have it for dessert."

"That's my girl!"

Ma wouldn't be sidetracked. "Some of them looked like boys, even younger than Randall. I can't imagine them with guns."

"That's how I feel about Andreas, the guy who works with me," I said.

"That where you both wrong," Pop told us. "They ain't just 'boys.' For one thing, they white. For another thing, they highly trained killers. Germany ain't conquered most o' Europe 'cause its soldiers can do kitchen work and enjoy some homemade cake! Maybe them fellas act all respectful and grateful when somebody give 'em a handout, but if *they* was in charge, it'd be way different. Then they'd be raping and killing and God only knows what else."

Voncille had said the same thing to Betty Jean.

"And you know who they go after first," Pop continued. "After they got rid of every Jew in America, they come after us."

"Their leaders have forced them to fight," Ma responded.

That's what Aunt Lou had said.

"I don't believe those young men would try to hurt us," Ma went on. "They just want to go home."

"Andreas hopes Germany loses the war," I said.

Pop turned on me. "I thought he can't speak no English."

"He's learned a little. On D-day, that's what he told us."

"And you believed him." Pop looked disgusted. "I reckon he know what side *his* bread buttered on. What you expect him to say? 'I hope we slaughter every last one o' yo' men tryin' to get a foothold in France'? Use your head, Caleb. He told y'all just what you wanted to hear."

"You always believe the worst," Ma said. "I guess you want our American boys to be just as bloodthirsty as you say the Germans are."

"Damn right I do! You think we gonna win this war by makin' nice? I didn't want us to fight, but now that we in it, now that Randall is over there, I want us to get the job done and get the hell out."

"Randall wouldn't hurt anyone unless he had to."

"Maybe not, but he better be ready to act without mercy if that time come. His life might depend on it. I hope they taught him *that*."

* * *

A couple days later we had heavy thunderstorms. Not many folks showed up at the Dixie Belle for breakfast, and so few turned up at dinnertime that Miss Sondra closed the place early.

Uncle Hiram had been having a bad time all morning.

Rainy weather made his rheumatism act up, and his hands ached. During the break after breakfast he soaked them in hot water, and Aunt Lou gave him some aspirin. But he was still in pain, and he dropped a bowl of potato salad because he couldn't make his fingers hold it tight enough.

After we closed up, Uncle Hiram went into the alley as he did most days, to smoke his pipe before the long process of cleaning up began. When Aunt Lou asked me to empty the garbage, I toted it into the alley. Uncle Hiram was leaning against the wall, rubbing his gnarled hands together. Tears were running down his face.

"Oh, Caleb!" He looked embarrassed and quickly wiped his eyes on his shirt sleeve.

I put down the can and went to him. "What's wrong, Uncle Hiram? Your hands still hurt?"

"Worse'n ever. They hurts so bad I can't hardly stand it no more. And I's so tired o' not bein' able to do my work the way I use to." He went back to rubbing his hands, like he was trying to push the pain and the stiffness out of them.

"I'm real sorry. Is there anything I can do?"

"No, son. Just please don't tell Lou I's out here actin' like a baby."

"All right. I'll tell her you're finishing your pipe."

"Thanks, Caleb. I be back in a minute, soon as I got hold o' myself."

The second I went through the door, I heard a voice say, "Caleb."

I didn't have to stop and think—or ask any questions. I knew.

No one else in the kitchen had heard anything. Andreas was bent over the sink, scrubbing a baking pan. Aunt Lou was dishing leftovers into a bowl. It was all so ordinary—and so unbelievable.

And now? I stopped and listened, but the only sounds were the regular noises of kitchen work. I had to do *something* for Uncle Hiram, but I realized that was for me to decide.

I went back into the alley and found Uncle Hiram in the same place, his forehead wet with sweat, his eyes closed tight. He jumped when I touched his arm.

"You back," he said. "Anything wrong?"

"No, nothing's wrong. I want to pray for you—ask God to fix your hands."

Uncle Hiram smiled, showing the empty places where teeth used to be. "Aw, honey, that's right sweet o' you. I shore could use some prayer."

I prayed to God every night, asking him to protect Randall, but this was different—personal. "What do I say?" I asked silently, but there was no answer. It was up to me.

Uncle Hiram held out his hands, palms up, like he expected me to put something in them. I took them in mine—gently, so I wouldn't add to his misery—and closed my eyes.

"Father in heaven, Uncle Hiram is hurting, hurting real bad. He . . . uh, he wants the pain to go away. And his hands to get back to the way they used to be, before the rheumatism got them so he can't do his work the way he used to."

"Oh, yes," said Uncle Hiram.

"So, Father, please touch Uncle Hiram's hands and heal them. Amen."

"Amen!" Uncle Hiram declared. "Thank you, honey. Thank you!"

We went back into the kitchen together to help the others finish cleaning up so we could all go home.

I walked through rain the whole way, but I didn't care. Being wet didn't matter. The lightning that cracked around me wasn't important either. Only one thing was on my mind: God had spoken to me again.

CHAPTER FOURTEEN

MA WAS SURPRISED to see me home early, and she fussed over me, which is just what I wanted. Soon I was in dry clothes, drinking a cup of coffee with lots of milk and sugar. She sat across the kitchen table from me, working on a pair of socks she was knitting for Randall.

"What is it?" Ma asked after a while. "What's wrong?"

"Nothing. I'm all right."

"You don't look all right. You have something on your mind. I can see it all over you. Things bad at the restaurant?"

I hadn't planned to say anything, but I plunged in.

"Ma, I've been wanting to tell you some things for a long time."

"You're not in trouble?"

"No, ma'am. At least I don't think so. But strange stuff has been happening to me—"

"I knew it! You haven't been acting quite yourself. Tell me."

"The day I got baptized . . . God spoke to me."

Ma dropped her knitting. "*God?* You're sure?"

I nodded. "Three times. The same thing each time."

"Why didn't you tell me? What did he say?" Ma's voice had dropped to a whisper.

"When I was under the water, God said my name and then 'Behold my servant.'"

Ma leaned toward me. "Then what happened?"

"I went home to change into dry clothes, remember?"

"Yes—"

"And I was in my bedroom, undressed, and a voice said the same thing. Real clear: 'Behold my servant.'"

"You heard it with your ears, the way you're hearing me now?"

"Yes, ma'am. I thought it was Nathan playing a joke. I looked everywhere, but no one was in the house with me. Then I heard it again, but not with my ears. It was like something coming from inside me, like an idea."

Ma folded her hands and rested her chin on them, like

she was getting ready to pray. "You haven't told any-one else?"

"Only Randall. He said it was just my imagination and I should forget it."

"But you know it wasn't."

"I thought about it a lot, and I can't figure anything else."

"Maybe when Grandpa blessed you, he gave you the gift of hearing from God."

That sounded pretty strange—spooky, even.

"I always knew there was something in you," Ma told me. "And now—"

"I don't like it!"

"Oh, son, why not? It's a rare blessing to have God speak to you."

Her words didn't help. "Please don't tell Pop."

Ma put a hand toward me, as if she wanted to make me stop and calm down. She looked thoughtful. "I understand about not telling your father. You're sure God said, 'Behold my servant'?"

"Yes. Why does God always want Negroes to be servants, Ma?"

She sighed. "Maybe God *doesn't* like how things are for us. But there are different ways to be a servant. Jesus washed the feet of his disciples at the Last Supper. That was a servant's job back in those days. He did it to show us how to serve one another."

That made sense. I was obeying God and serving Uncle Hiram at the same time. I told Ma about hearing the voice and then praying for Uncle Hiram.

Ma reached across the table and put her hand on mine. "This is important, Caleb. What's happened to you, I mean. Understand?"

"Yes, ma'am."

"Your father really should know, even if—"

"No! He'd just make fun of me. *Please* don't tell him!"

She sighed. "All right. We'll wait."

* * *

Pop came home all steamed up about how he'd been short-changed at the hardware store. He went on about it over supper, and then he got on to some bad war news from the Pacific. He didn't ask about my day or anything, and that suited me fine.

After supper I answered a knock at the door. There stood Aunt Lou and Uncle Hiram.

"Uncle Hiram?" Ma said. "Aunt Lou? Are y'all okay? Please, come in the house."

They didn't move. "A miracle done happened!" Uncle Hiram cried.

Pop joined us at the door. "Uncle Hiram, what is it?"

"Show 'em," Aunt Lou said.

Uncle Hiram held out his hands. The fingers weren't all pressed up against one another, tilted at that crazy angle toward his little fingers, the way they used to be. They were still an old man's hands, but the fingers were almost straight. His knuckles and joints looked normal, too—no more swelling.

"Looka here," he said, flexing his fingers. The words came faster and faster. "My rheumatism—no! I ain't gonna call it *mine* no more, it warn't *ever* mine, but a curse the devil put on me—that damn old rheumatism is *gone!* God done took it outta my body and sent it as far from me as east is from the west. Caleb prayed to God, askin' him to heal me, and God done heard his prayer!"

Uncle Hiram grabbed my hands and held them tight. His hands were strong now—the hands of a man who'd used them for hard work all his life.

"Oh, Lord Jesus!" Ma cried.

"Caleb prayed for me this afternoon, and God done healed me! Thank you, honey! Oh, thank you, God!" He put his hands over his face, and his shoulders began to heave.

Suddenly my head felt all squeezy, and I had to sit down.

"I'll get some water," I heard Ma say.

When my head cleared, Uncle Hiram and Aunt Lou were sitting on the settee, holding hands. Pop stood by the front door, his arms crossed.

Ma wiped my forehead with a damp cloth, and I felt better.

"Tell your mama and daddy how it happened," Uncle Hiram said.

I glanced at Pop. I didn't like the deep wrinkle between his eyes, but I went ahead and told the story again.

After I finished, Ma asked Uncle Hiram, "When did you truly get healed?"

"It didn't happen right off. Lou and me went home, just like Caleb did, and we was wet to our skins, even though we had a umbrella. Wind was so bad, nothin' could o' kept us dry."

"I put on the kettle right away," Aunt Lou said, "and sent Hiram to change into dry things. When I come to the bedroom to tell him the tea was ready, he was sound asleep, quilt pulled up over him, so I let him be."

"While I was asleep, I had the most wonderful dream!" Uncle Hiram was smiling as he remembered. "I was sittin' on my porch swing. Jasmine was bloomin' all 'long the fence, and honeysuckle on the porch pillars. Bees hummin' everywhere. And while I's sittin' there, here come a man up the porch steps, and right away I knowed it was a angel."

"An angel!" Ma exclaimed. "What did he look like?"

"Just like you, Frank," Uncle Hiram replied. "Big, strong fella."

"Like me?" Pop looked like he was trying to hold back a smile. "If you say so."

"He did indeed," Uncle Hiram said warmly.

"The angel was a Negro?" Ma asked.

Uncle Hiram nodded. "Dressed in a blue work shirt and overalls."

A warm, tingly feeling was creeping up my backbone, and I felt lightheaded again. But then I remembered: it was just a dream. Anything was possible in a dream.

"What happened next?" Ma asked.

"He sit down 'side me and took out a little bottle from his bib pocket. Then he opened it and poured out some oil onto my hands and begun to rub it into my fingers and knuckles. It smelled so sweet, it put that ol' jasmine and honeysuckle to shame! And soon as he begun to work it in, my hands started gettin' warm. It felt right good. Seem like it lasted a long time. I don't recollect anything after that, but when I woke up, my hands was healed!"

He held up both hands and turned them one way and another, like he had to prove to himself it was true.

I looked over at Pop, wondering what he was thinking. He was in the same place, arms still folded, looking at Uncle Hiram the way you might look at a two-headed mule.

Ma broke the silence. "Uncle Hiram, we're so happy for you. A miracle! Right here in Toad Hop. Oh"—she went to him and took his hands in hers—"I can hardly believe it!"

"Me either, honey," he told her. "I thought I was gonna have to wait until I come to glory to get back my hands like they use to be. But now . . ." He got to his feet. "I got to go outside, get myself together. I know y'all don't want to watch a old man bawl like a baby."

"This calls for a celebration," Ma said. "Aunt Lou, why don't you come in the kitchen and help me get some cake and coffee together?"

Uncle Hiram went past Pop onto the porch, and Ma and Aunt Lou went into the kitchen. That left Pop and me. I kept my eyes down, but I knew his were fixed on me.

"So," Pop began. "You prayed for him and his hands got 'healed' while he was takin' his nap?"

"I guess so—I mean, yes, sir."

"And you believe *God* healed him? *Because* you prayed?" Pop asked the questions like he was trying to get things straight in his own mind.

I had to be careful now, or we'd get into a fight, and I didn't want that. "All I know is that I prayed for him after work, and what he just told us. That's all. I'm—surprised, too."

"You believe God healed him *because* you prayed?"

How many more times was Pop going to ask me that?

"I told you. I prayed for him and now his hands are all right. I don't know if God healed him because I prayed. Maybe God was going to do it anyway. I don't know."

Ma came back into the room, a tray in her hands. "Frank, let Uncle Hiram know we've got some pound cake and coffee ready."

I was off the hook, at least for a while. But after he finished his cake, Uncle Hiram said, "Ain't every day God give one o' his children the gift of healin', like he done with Brother Caleb here."

Brother Caleb? That was a title reserved for the older men of the church.

"—and they's plenty o' folks what needs healin' even more'n I did." Uncle Hiram held up his hands yet again, staring at them like he'd never seen them before. "We got to tell 'em, get 'em over here so's Caleb can pray for 'em."

"Hold on, now," Pop told him. "Slow down a bit. Just because y'all think that Caleb might of had somethin' to do with all this ain't no reason to start up a sideshow in town."

"Frank!" Ma exclaimed.

Pop's eyebrows went up the way they did when he was irritated. "I don't mean no disrespect, Uncle Hiram, but once word get out that my boy is a so-called healer, we gonna have a circus on our hands. That ain't gonna happen if I can stop it."

I felt irritated. Why didn't Pop ask me what *I* wanted to do?

Uncle Hiram looked hurt. "You don't wanna deny folks they healin' if God really *has* done picked Caleb to be his chosen vessel, does you, Frank?"

"I don't know about all that. But I do know that Caleb ain't gonna be billed in town as no miracle worker."

"Wait a minute," I said. "Nobody's saying that."

Pop ignored me. "It ain't fair to him or anyone else. Even if they is some connection between him prayin' for you and what happen to your hands, ain't no guarantee it would happen again."

"But no one will ever know unless Caleb is allowed to try," Ma retorted.

Pop ignored her, too. "I won't have you sayin' that Caleb prayed for you," he told Uncle Hiram. "Of course you got to tell everyone about your hands—"

"Nothin' could keep him quiet 'bout that!" Aunt Lou exclaimed.

"—but please leave Caleb out of it," Pop finished.

"Isn't that for Caleb to decide?" Ma said.

"Ma's right," I declared.

Pop looked at me. "Not while you livin' under my roof. I ain't gonna have no religious craziness here with you at the center."

"I hears you," Uncle Hiram told Pop. "I don't agree with you, Frank, but I hears you. Ain't nobody gonna find out from me how the Lord done answered Caleb's prayer."

Once Uncle Hiram and Aunt Lou had left, I wanted to get off by myself before I blew up at Pop. Yeah, part of me was glad he spoke up. I was scared by the idea of folks knowing that God had answered my prayer for Uncle Hiram. I could imagine a line of people in the yard—the blind, the deaf, the crippled—trying to grab on to me, begging me to pray and heal them. I didn't want to be responsible for getting folks healed . . . or blamed if they didn't get better.

But I was mad, too. Pop could have asked me about it instead of taking over like it was his duty—his *right*—to run my life.

Pop took up a newspaper. Ma tidied the kitchen, and I sat and stewed.

Just when I was ready to go to my room, Ma came back and sat down by me. "Today wasn't the first time God spoke to Caleb," she said to Pop.

I didn't want to open this up again. "Ma!"

"Your father *has* to know. It started the day he got baptized, Frank."

Pop put down his paper. "What did?"

"God *spoke* to Caleb that day. Three times. Tell him, son."

I kept quiet. The minute I said another word, the fight would begin.

"You heard your ma." Pop sounded resigned. "Let's hear the whole story so we can get it over with."

So much for what *I* wanted. "Ma's right. When I was under the water, God called my name and said, 'Behold my servant.' Then he said the same thing two more times when I was in the bedroom, changing clothes."

"*God* talked to you."

"Yes, sir."

"And you believe that, Lucy?"

"I do, Frank."

"And you both believe that because Caleb prayed for Hiram, God healed his hands."

We said we did.

"But *you* don't," Ma said to Pop. She had made this *her* fight now.

"No, sugar, I don't."

"But you can't deny that Uncle Hiram's hands are . . . *different* from what they were." Ma was choosing her words carefully.

"They are different. I allow that."

"But how do you *explain* it?"

"I can't," Pop admitted. "But they's lots o' things in this world I can't explain—can't *nobody* explain. The man's hands is better—that's the important thing."

"So you don't believe in the power of prayer? That God answers prayer and heals because people pray?"

I wanted to say *Pop doesn't even believe in God* but knew better.

I expected some kind of wisecrack, but Pop answered seriously. "Y'all might not believe me, but I give this a lot o' thought over the years, and in all honesty, I can't say that I do. I allow that prayer can help some folks *feel* better about things. Some folks need to believe they's a God in heaven who can help 'em, who might . . . *do* things for 'em. But life done taught me one thing, and the sooner Caleb learns it the better: a man got to do for *hisself* if he want anything in this world. And that's doubly true for the Negro man."

Ma was upset, I could tell, but she didn't raise her voice. "What about Negro women?"

"It ain't as important for women. They got men to look after 'em. That's the way it suppose to be. If a woman want to pray, ain't no harm in it."

Ma shook her head wearily.

Pop paused, like he was considering what to say next. "Probably ain't no harm in a man prayin', either. Long as he don't depend on the idea about a God doin' for him what he got to do for hisself."

"Then I suppose you think I'm wasting time praying for Randall!"

"Not if it give you strength to keep goin'."

"I don't care about my *strength*. I care about my *son!* I care about him coming home safely. I care about him not being killed!" Ma's voice got louder and louder. "And let me tell you something else, Frank Brown. As sure as I know anything, I know there's a God, and he's in heaven, and he hears our prayers. He spoke to Caleb the day he was baptized, and his Spirit moved Caleb to pray for Uncle Hiram, and he heard Caleb's prayer, and that's why that man is healed. If none of that's true, then I don't want to go on living in this world!"

Never in my life had I heard Ma talk to Pop like that. Pop looked shocked. Love for Ma surged through me, and I looked at her with new respect.

"Sugar, I didn't mean to upset you," said Pop. "But you and Caleb got to realize—"

"The thing I realize right now is how sorry I am for you. Life must be so hard when you don't have anything to believe in."

For once, Pop didn't have an answer, and I saw my chance. "You didn't explain what you think happened when I got baptized."

"Looks like I already done said too much. We best let it go."

I wasn't about to. "No. Tell me, Pop! I have lots of questions and no answers. Explain it to me so I can understand."

"All right, then." He took a deep breath. "You thought you heard from God 'cause o' your need to make yourself look important."

"That's unfair!" Ma exclaimed.

"Hold on, now. I ain't sayin' you done it on purpose, Caleb. But the mind is a funny thing. Maybe they was somethin' deep inside you, feelin' bad for all the messes you been makin' these past years, and to help you feel better, it gave you somethin' to hold on to. Somethin' to . . . believe in."

"No, Pop. He *did* speak to me. I heard him."

"The mind can make us see things that ain't really there, hear voices nobody else can hear, believe unbelievable things, too. If you could go back in time and ask Ol' Nat Turner if he saw it rain black blood back in eighteen thirty-one, he tell you yes. Sister Johnson swear on a stack o' Bibles that Jesus show himself to her in a vision one day while she was boilin' laundry. Remember that, Lucy? Nobody can say she didn't see Jesus, but where her proof?"

"We can't expect that kind of proof," Ma answered sadly. She had calmed down now and looked bone tired.

Pop didn't argue that point. "If Caleb say that God spoke to him, I can't deny he believe it. If y'all believe that Uncle Hiram is healed 'cause God work a miracle, so be it. Like I said, the important thing is that the man's hands is normal now. What's it matter how it happened?"

"And what about what God said to Caleb? What does that mean?"

"How should I know? Nobody said nothin' to *me*, remember?"

"So you still don't believe?"

"No, sugar. They's been times when I wished I could, but I can't."

For the first time I could ever remember, I felt sorry for Pop.

Ma said nothing more.

Pop got up. "We see things different, Lucy, and that's all they is to it. Maybe it would be better if we all agreed about this stuff, but I don't see that happening."

Ma got up, too. She rubbed her hand over my head the way she used to do when I was little. "I love you, son," she said. "And I'm proud of you."

Then she went to bed, and Pop said he was going to sit on the porch. He said I was welcome to sit with him while he smoked his pipe, but I stayed inside. I had to be alone.

In the darkness of my room I tried to pray, but no words would come. I went back over everything that had happened that day, trying to remember the words I'd said when I prayed for Uncle Hiram. I couldn't. Then the questions came again, questions with no answers.

CHAPTER FIFTEEN

I COULDN'T SLEEP, so I pulled on clothes and went out the window. It didn't take much to rouse Nathan, and soon we were at the creek. I told him everything, beginning with praying for Uncle Hiram. I *had* to tell someone—someone who wasn't Pop, who didn't believe anything, or Ma, who believed everything.

I half expected Nathan to make a bunch of smart comments, but he didn't.

"Remember the day we got baptized and I accused you of hiding in my house and playing that joke on me?" I asked him.

"Yeah, but I didn't pay you much mind, 'cause I thought *you* was messin' with *me*."

"I kind of wish that's all it was."

"It be a lot simpler all around if it wasn't the Lord God who decided to call you out. So what happens now?"

"I wish I knew!"

"You gonna share your secret with anybody else? I know someone who'd be right curious about it."

"Henry?"

"Yeah. And maybe his daddy'll let him be friends again, now that you gone and become such a holy man."

"Don't say that! I'm just the same as always."

It was too dark to see Nathan's face clearly, but I could sense him looking at me.

"No, you ain't, Caleb."

"What?"

"You ain't the same. If God been talkin' to you, workin' a healing through you—you ain't the same."

"Be serious! You don't believe all that stuff."

"I am bein' serious. Wish I could say it's just a bunch of . . . you know, but I can't."

"Why not?"

"'Cause I can't figure a better explanation. And . . ."

"And what?"

"And 'cause *you* believe everything you just told me."

For some reason, that made me feel better.

"You reckon Uncle Hiram's gonna keep quiet about you prayin' for him?"

"I hope so. Pop was dead set against him saying anything."

"Your daddy is probably doin' you a favor. Once word get out that you 'got the gift,' you'd be famous."

"No, thanks. It's better this way."

"But you wouldn't hold back from prayin' for someone who *did* know your secret?"

"Only six people know it, including me and you."

"That's what I mean." He stood up and started to unbutton his pants. "You see, I got this nasty ol' boil on my ass, and I thought that if you'd lay hands on it and—"

I threw a handful of wet sand at him. "Very funny."

"Seriously, man. If Uncle Hiram can't keep quiet—"

"He will. He promised Pop he wouldn't talk."

"You'll find out tomorrow morning, I reckon. Everybody at the Dixie Belle is gonna see right off that his hands is different."

"I know. But Uncle Hiram doesn't have to say *how* it happened except that he prayed and God did a miracle."

"And you standin' there bitin' your tongue. That gonna be hard for you."

"No, it won't! Why should it?"

"Jeez, Caleb. I *know* you, remember? You did somethin' good—somethin' real good—and naturally you want some credit. Who wouldn't?"

"God gets the credit, not me."

"Whatever you say." He was quiet for a minute, then: "You mind if I touch you?"

He was going to mess with me again, but suddenly I wasn't sure if he was serious or not.

"Why do you want to do that?"

"'Cause I never touched no saint before, and maybe some o' your holiness can rub off on me. God knows I could use it."

I threw more sand at him, and he threw some back at me, and after a while we were both so dirty we had to skinny-dip in Hale's Pond to get cleaned up before we went home.

On the way back past the church, Nathan suggested we stop by Henry's and see if he'd come out. I reminded him that Henry wasn't supposed to see us, but Nathan argued it was way past time for that nonsense to stop. I agreed, so we knocked at Henry's window and asked him if he wanted to hang out with us.

He came out, and I told him the story of what had happened since our baptism day. Henry was impressed—and ready to have a reason to make up. He apologized for not coming out nights to join us even though his daddy had told him not to. Then he blamed himself for not listening to Jesus' command about not judging others lest you be judged, and Nathan threatened to punch him unless he dropped all that holy talk. Henry realized Nathan was joking—I wasn't so sure—and we all agreed that from now on we were friends again.

* * *

At the Dixie Belle the next day, Uncle Hiram showed off what he kept calling his "new hands" to everyone. Miss Sondra seemed to be impressed and said she was glad— anyone would be happy to see another person free from pain, and she wished someone could do something for her sciatica. Andreas was pleased, and he and Uncle Hiram got a little game going; every time they went by each other, they had to shake hands. Betty Jean smiled and said nothing much, and Voncille acted like she couldn't understand what all the fuss was about.

Uncle Hiram winked at me, like we were two insiders on a private joke. And Aunt Lou—she kissed my cheek when she saw me, thanked me again, and told me she was proud to know me. I found a huge piece of pecan pie waiting for me after the dinner dishes were finished, too.

It felt strange not being able to say anything. I had to be honest with myself: I *did* want some credit for Uncle Hiram's healing. Nathan was right: anybody would. And what was wrong with that?

* * *

When I got home that afternoon, Ma was in the sitting room, holding her Bible. "I found what I was looking for," she said when I came in. "Sit down and let me show you.

'Behold my servant' is in Isaiah, chapter forty-two. I should have remembered. Daddy used to quote it."

I took the Bible and started to read: "'Behold my servant, whom I uphold; mine elect, in whom my soul delighteth; I have put my spirit upon him: he shall bring forth judgment to the Gentiles.'" My eyes skipped down the page. "'To open the blind eyes, to bring out the prisoners from the prison, and them that sit in darkness out of the prison house.'"

"Right there," Ma said. "That verse: 'to bring out the prisoners from the prison.' When your grandpa was a young man, about your age, he got together with some of his friends and made a plan to rescue two black men from being hanged. They'd been accused of raping a white woman, and they were being held in the county jail."

I thought I'd heard all the old family stories, but this was news to me. "Here? In Davisville?"

"No—somewhere on the other side of the state. He would never tell me where."

"What happened?"

"The men were being held—for trial, is what the sheriff told folks, but your grandpa said everyone knew they were going to be taken out of the jail at night and lynched. Your grandpa and his friends got there first, and they freed those men. Saved their lives!"

"So Grandpa was a hero."

"I always thought so, but *he* didn't. He just said he was obeying God. And he paid a price, too: he had to leave the county, change his name, and never go back. To this day, I don't know my own daddy's real given name or where he came from. That's why we don't have any family on Daddy's side—just Mama's folks." I had never thought about that.

"Does this have something to do with what God said to me?"

She nodded. "I believe the same call God put on your grandpa's life is on yours now."

"I could never do anything like what Grandpa did."

Ma smiled. "I don't guess he ever imagined such a thing, either. But when the time came, he obeyed."

"What can *I* do, Ma?"

"Whatever God calls you to. Randall's off fighting for freedom in Europe. You're too young to be drafted, thank God, but that doesn't mean you're not called to fight here."

"Fight who? The only person I ever fight with is Pop."

Ma grimaced. "Don't forget the Hill boys."

"That's different."

"I know. But think about it. There are different enemies out there, Caleb, and different ways to fight them."

I didn't know what to say.

Ma saw me hesitating. "You don't need all the answers just now." She put her Bible in my hands. "Read this again, or look it up in Grandpa's Bible. Be patient. God will help you know what to do next. He's not finished with you yet."

I let that sink in for a moment. Then my mind went back to last night. "Can I ask you a question, Ma?"

"Of course."

"About what you said to Pop last night—about how you believe in God, and prayer, and all that stuff."

Ma raised an eyebrow. "My so-called stand of faith?"

"Yeah. You sure laid it on the line with Pop. Is he mad at you?"

Now Ma smiled a little. "More surprised than mad, maybe. Your father hasn't heard many such speeches from me over the years."

I put my hand on Ma's. "What you said was great. I was real proud of you."

"Why, thank you, Caleb. Let's hope it gives your father something to think about. After all, we never know how what we say or do can change another person's life." Ma got a faraway look in her eyes. Then she looked at me. "But you know that now, don't you?"

"Yes, ma'am."

"Don't worry about your father and me. We disagree sometimes—lots of times, in fact—but we couldn't get along without each other."

I was surprised at how relieved I felt.

CHAPTER SIXTEEN

WHEN I THOUGHT about folks in Toad Hop who needed healing—little Diamond Swan with his clubfoot, Aunt Ruthie Green with her bad heart, even Miss Suzy Jackson with her back problems—I wondered if I should offer to pray for them. Or if God would speak to me and tell me to pray for them. There were so many hurting people. Most of them didn't have any money to go to a doctor, and even if they could pay, the only doctor who would treat Negroes lived in Waynesboro, a long morning's wagon ride away.

Uncle Hiram kept his promise not to say anything about me. After a few days the excitement about his hands started to wear off, and before long it seemed like they had always been healed. That's how fast most folks forgot.

The Dixie Belle was all right now—I was used to it. Andreas practiced his English on us, and we found out that he did have a family in Germany, parents and a sister. They knew he was a POW and that he was at Camp Davis, safe, because the Red Cross had informed them. We also learned that his older brother, Reinhardt, had been killed fighting in North Africa. I was sure he was grieving, even though he didn't let on.

Then one morning Andreas didn't come to work. Or the next day, or the next. The fourth day, he was back. His face was a mess of purple and yellow bruises, and several dark stitches held his lower lip together.

"Lord Jesus, what done happen to you?" Aunt Lou exclaimed. "You look like you been beaten to a pulp."

He wouldn't say anything.

Miss Sondra told us to get to work, that Andreas was all right now and what had happened was none of our business.

Lee Davis showed up after breakfast, sent Andreas into the dining room to sweep, and talked to the rest of us. "Seems they got some crazy Nazis in that camp," he began. "That's what Colonel Ross told me. Fanatics—swore blood oaths to Hitler and the party, that kind of nonsense. Ross says they been terrorizing the camp, 'specially other prisoners who don't share their ideas. And they've been laying for Andreas."

I wanted to ask why the people who ran the camp couldn't protect Andreas, but I wouldn't interrupt a white man.

"He told us back on D-day that he want Germany to *lose* the war," Uncle Hiram exclaimed.

Davis shook his head. "From what Ross told me, he ain't the only one that feels like that. I reckon a lot of them fellows just want the war to be over so they can go home. That's how I'd feel if I was in their shoes. Anyway, that's the situation."

Aunt Lou looked worried. "Ain' they some way to protect him? Them bad ones is sure to come lookin' for him again."

"Ross is taking care of that. Some of the worst ones is gonna be sent to a higher-security camp. In the meantime Ross says they're gonna assign some extra guards in the camp, make sure no one else gets beat up."

"No way they can protect that child," Aunt Lou said, "unless they put him off somewhere by hisself—or post a guard to stand by his bed every night."

"I feel bad for him," said Betty Jean.

"Me, too," said Uncle Hiram. "He only a young man. You can tell by lookin' at him that he can't defend hisself."

"What's wrong with y'all?" Voncille cried. "It's our *en-*

emies you're talkin' about. The sooner *all* of them is gone, the better."

Davis tried to calm her down, but Voncille said she had her work to do and couldn't waste any more time listening to something that wasn't any of her concern.

When we were done for the day, Andreas joined me in the alley for our meal, as usual. Aunt Lou had put enough food on his plate to feed three people, and there was a huge piece of chocolate cake, too. For the first time that day, he smiled.

I wished I could talk to him better, really learn more about what had happened, get to know him. So I tried. "I'm sorry you got beat up."

He didn't understand.

"You know—hit." I punched myself lightly on the face.

"Ah. *Ein Prügel.* A . . . beat—"

"Beating. I'm sorry."

He shrugged. "Thank you."

"Aren't you afraid to go back to the camp?" I made what I hoped was a scared-looking face.

Andreas nodded. "Yes. A lot. *Aber*—" He shrugged again, like there was nothing to be done about it.

"Davis told us that the bad ones are being sent away. He says you're going to be protected. He says there'll be extra security." I knew Andreas couldn't follow me, but I was saying it for myself, not for him. I wanted it all to be true.

He touched my arm. "*Danke*. You . . . how do I say it?" He tapped his forehead.

"Oh. Understand. I get it."

"*Ja*. You understand."

"I want to."

"Hitler, Nazis . . . they do bad things. I want . . . America . . . win the war."

"You told me that a long time ago."

"I say this . . . in the camp, and . . ." He pointed to his swollen lip.

"You shouldn't say anything! Keep it to yourself."

"*Wie?*"

I put my finger to my lips and shook my head.

He smiled, but he looked serious. "*Ich muss*—I must—*die Wahrheit sagen*. You understand? *Verstehst du?*"

"No, I don't, but you have to keep quiet. Make them protect you!"

Andreas put down his plate. "I show you . . . a thing." He pulled up his T-shirt to reveal his skinny chest. Purple bruises covered his ribs. Just above his left nipple, over the heart, he'd been branded.

A swastika, blood red, blazed against his pale skin.

"Jesus! Who did that? The ones who beat you up?"

"Yes. To . . ."

"Hurt you?"

He nodded.

"And to punish you for telling the truth!" Now it was clear.

Next time they might kill him.

For telling the truth. For doing what he believed was right.

Suddenly I saw Andreas in a new way. He was someone I could respect.

Even though he was a German soldier.

Andreas picked up his dessert and held it toward me. "Here. *Zuviel für mich*—you eat, too."

So we ate Aunt Lou's chocolate cake together—from the same plate.

* * *

Randall had gotten to Naples safely, which was good, because the German U-boats in the Atlantic were dangerous. But northern Italy was still held by the Germans, who had built forts there—the Gothic Line, Pop had told me. Our guys had orders to break through and drive the German army north out of Italy. It would be a hard job. The Germans had built their forts on mountaintops, and Pop said it was hell to attack an enemy firing down at you.

For the first time, I was panicky with worry. Nights were worst, when I had nothing else to think about. I'd look at Randall's empty bed and wonder what he was doing— still sleeping, probably, since Italy was six or seven hours ahead of us. Had he marched that day, or fought, or just sat somewhere waiting for something to happen? Had he met any Germans? Had he killed any?

Randall's letters came less and less often, and by the end of July, there were none.

Then at last we had something to celebrate. The power lines were all strung, and the electricity was finally turned on. Pop had been saving his money, and he had our place wired. One outlet in each room, and one light bulb hanging from each ceiling. So we were ready. Ma had bought a floor lamp for the sitting room, and that first night, we pulled our chairs around it and read. Pop had his new issue of *Life,* Ma her Bible, and I was paging through the funny papers of the Sunday paper.

"I never thought I'd see this day," Ma declared. "Some folks in Toad Hop can't afford electricity, and others that can won't go to the trouble."

"We been livin' in the dark ages way too long," Pop agreed.

"And just think! That iron we ordered from Sears and Roebuck will be here any day. I can't wait to throw out those heavy old flatirons."

"I got something else for you," Pop said. "Wait a minute." He left the room and came back with a box wrapped in pretty paper.

Ma opened it carefully. "A radio! How sweet. Plug it in."

"We got to unplug the lamp, then."

The radio began to glow as it warmed up. Then there was static, but as Pop fiddled with the tuning knob, suddenly there was music. In a moment, it sounded like Louis Armstrong and his orchestra were right in the room.

"Oh, Frank! What a wonderful present."

"Care to dance, Mrs. Brown?"

"I'd be delighted, Mr. Brown."

Pop took Ma in his arms and began dancing her around the room. After that, Ma made coffee and served us some peach pie. For that moment, my life was good. I had a full belly, a roof over my head, music on the radio, and folks who loved each other and weren't ragging on me.

But the worries came back. Not too far away, Andreas was in his barracks, maybe wondering when the next attack would come. And Randall—where was he tonight, and how was he? Asleep in a foxhole, cold, tired, under fire? Was it right that Pop and Ma were dancing, that we were eating pie and laughing together, when so many others were lonely or in danger?

CHAPTER SEVENTEEN

Dinner was extra busy the next day, and things began to go wrong. Betty Jean dropped a platter of sliced tomatoes, and Voncille snapped at her for being so clumsy. Then a table for ten came in, businessmen passing through on their way to Augusta, saying they were in a hurry and needed especially fast service. While we were scrambling to fill ten orders at once, Voncille brought back a plate of food from a regular customer, who had complained that the beans were too salty, the gravy cold, and the biscuits too brown.

Andreas and I rushed to keep the clean dishes coming. At last Aunt Lou and Uncle Hiram had the businessmen's plates all ready. Voncille stacked her serving tray, picked it up, and started for the dining room. Then she noticed her apron was untied in the back.

"Somebody help me here!" she called. "I can't go out there like this."

I dried my hands and went to help her. But Voncille stopped me. "Not *you*. Andreas, come tie this apron."

For a second, he just looked at her.

"Come *on!*" she cried. "This food ain't gettin' any hotter."

He looked at me, then went over to her, fumbled with the strings of the apron, and managed to tie a clumsy bow.

"Thanks," she said, and walked out without even turning around.

Andreas went back to the sink, but I stayed where I was.

"Caleb?" Aunt Lou called. "What is it?"

Uncle Hiram looked up from the potatoes he was mashing.

"Sugar, what'sa matter?" Aunt Lou asked.

Voncille hurried back in. "Hiram, you got more sweet tea ready?" Then she noticed me. "What are you standing there for?"

Fear and anger had been going after each other inside me like two starved dogs fighting over a bone. Anger won. Voncille had treated me like dirt long enough, and I wasn't going to let it pass—not anymore. "Why wouldn't you let me tie your apron?"

"What?"

"Why wouldn't you let me tie your apron?"

It had gotten very quiet in the kitchen.

"Don't you speak to me that way!"

"You didn't want *me* to tie your apron."

"Get back to your work and let me get back to mine."

"You hate Andreas, but you'd rather let him near you than someone like me."

"You can think whatever you damn well please. I'm tired o' tryin' to guess what crazy stuff goes on inside a nigger's head." She slammed through the door and came back in a moment with Lee Davis.

"What's goin' on in here?" he demanded. "Don't y'all see we got a full house today? This ain't no time for y'all to be squabbling."

"I won't work in a place where the nigger help can talk back to me," Voncille said. "You get rid of him, or I'm leavin'."

"Caleb, what'd you say to Miss Voncille?"

I could feel every eye on me. "I asked why she'd let Andreas tie her apron but not me."

"That's *it?* That's what all this is about?"

"He sassed me, Mr. Lee!" Voncille said. "I don't have to put up with that."

Davis looked at me. "Caleb, if you want your job, you apologize to Miss Voncille. If you won't, then you can consider yourself fired."

"If *he* go, Hiram and me go with him!" Aunt Lou announced.

I wanted to walk out and not look back. But then I'd have to explain things to Pop. Maybe Davis would come by the house and tell him how I'd mouthed off to a white woman; then there'd be hell to pay.

I had to think about Aunt Lou and Uncle Hiram, too. They didn't like working at the Dixie Belle, and Aunt Lou said lots of times she wished she could go back to Lee Davis's kitchen, but if she quit the restaurant, maybe he wouldn't take her back.

"Caleb?" Davis said, and I realized I'd been deep in my thoughts.

"I mean it about quittin'," Aunt Lou went on. "All Caleb axed for was a explanation."

"I don't owe that boy a thing," Voncille declared. "'Specially not an explanation. Everybody understands how things work. A white woman doesn't have to put up with"—she eyed me coldly—"a *colored* boy touching her. It's never been that way, and it ain't going to start being that way now."

The way she said *colored* made the word sound worse than the other one.

Everyone was still looking at me. I was sweating, and not because it was hot in the kitchen.

"Well?" Lee Davis asked. "We ain't got all day."

"Just fire him, Mr. Lee," Voncille urged. "He been nothin' but trouble since day one."

"That's not true!" I protested before I could stop myself.

"You hush, Caleb!" Davis ordered. "The only thing I want to hear from your mouth is an apology, and I want to hear it now."

"If he don't, I'm through here," Voncille declared.

"Where else you gonna find a job," Aunt Lou asked, "seein' as how you can't do nothin' 'cept pick up plates and pour sweet tea?"

"Y'all stop!" Davis cried. "Caleb, this is your last chance. You gonna apologize or not?"

The thought of apologizing made me sick, but I realized I was going to do it anyway. I wanted to believe it was to save Aunt Lou's and Uncle Hiram's jobs, but it wasn't. I'd been angry just a moment ago, but now I was plain scared— of Pop, of Davis, of what might happen if I refused. Knowing *that* made me want to run into the alley and cry.

I could only hope my words sounded sincere. "Miss Voncille, I'm sorry for what I said."

She just glared at me.

"There, you see?" Davis told her. "He apologized. You satisfied?"

Of course she wasn't—only getting rid of me could do that. But now *she* was under the gun. She'd told Betty Jean how much she needed her job.

"I reckon," she said. "But you tell him not to speak to me again."

"All right. You understand, Caleb?"

"Yes, sir."

"That's bein' sensible. Now can y'all *please* go back to work?" With that, he went through the door. And the machine known as the kitchen of the Dixie Belle Café started back up. After all, the folks in the dining room needed their sweet tea and their banana pudding.

CHAPTER EIGHTEEN

JUST BEFORE CLOSING TIME, Joe Peters, Lee Davis's handyman, knocked on the back door and asked for Aunt Lou. She talked to him a minute and then gestured for me to come.

"Miz Katie sent Joe over with this—for you." She handed me a sealed envelope. I wiped my hands, opened it, and read aloud, "'Caleb, please come by The Cedars today after work. There is something I need to discuss with you. Mrs. Katie Davis.'"

After what had happened earlier, the note worried me. "Am I in trouble?"

"Can't say, sugar," Aunt Lou said. "You done anything might make her mad?"

"No. I've never even talked to her."

"Maybe she got some extra work for you to do 'round her place. That's what white folks usually want."

"I don't want to go."

"Can't say I blame you. But you better. You already been in enough hot water for one day."

"Yes, ma'am. I know."

"That Voncille is one snippy bitch! I reckon it was right hard to apologize, warn't it?"

"Yes, ma'am."

"You didn't mean it."

"No, ma'am."

"I wouldn't have, either." Aunt Lou sighed. "Look like we colored folks spend way too much time sayin' things to white folks that we don't really mean."

"You always tell Lee Davis what you think! I've heard you."

She frowned, like she was thinking hard. "Sometimes. But it don't come easy."

"I think you're brave."

Aunt Lou patted my arm. "I 'preciate that, sugar, but I ain't nowhere near as brave as I'd like to be. I hopes to see the day we can say what we want without havin' to *be* brave."

I tried to imagine a world like that.

"Listen to me runnin' on!" Aunt Lou exclaimed. "You git, now. Find out what Miz Katie want with you. We can take care o' things here."

* * *

The Cedars, a big white house with columns, stood a mile on the far side of Davisville, just off the main road up toward Waynesboro and Augusta. Aunt Minnie, who cooked for the Davises now that Aunt Lou was at the Dixie Belle, answered the kitchen door. She'd been expecting me and had angel food cake with peaches and cold milk ready.

While I ate, Aunt Minnie went to tell Miss Katie I was there and then came back and said for me to follow her.

This was my first time inside The Cedars, and now I understood why folks said it was like a king's palace. Big pieces of carved furniture stood against the walls, which were papered in fancy designs. Portraits of people in old-fashioned clothes hung among paintings of racehorses. Thick rugs with bright patterns covered the shiny wood floors, and there were sparkly electric lights hanging from the ceilings.

In the front parlor, Miss Katie waited for me next to an old lady in a bathrobe, slumped in a wheelchair. Her head drooped on her chest, and she looked to be asleep.

"Thank you, Minnie," Miss Katie said. "I'll ring when we're done."

My heart was beating fast, and I wished I was somewhere else. Aunt Lou had made me wash up, but my pants were stained with food, and my shirt was wet under the arms.

"Thank you for coming," she said.

I kept my eyes down. "Yes, ma'am."

"This is Miss Evelyn, Mr. Lee's mother. She's been staying with us for a while now."

"Yes, ma'am. I done heard that."

"And perhaps you've heard that Miss Evelyn's mind is . . . no longer clear."

"I done heard that, too, ma'am, and I mighty sorry 'bout it."

"Thank you. You probably wonder why I've asked you here this afternoon."

I nodded. "I shore do hope I ain't . . . in no trouble."

"Oh, no, it's nothing like that. Did my message worry you?"

"Maybe a little bit, ma'am."

"I'm so sorry. Let me explain. I heard from Minnie that Uncle Hiram's been telling her how you prayed for his hands to be healed, and they were. Is that correct?"

So he hadn't been able to keep our secret! That bothered me, but it was too late to do anything about it now. "That right, Miz Katie. I prayed for him, and the Lord done the rest."

"I believe you. I've seen Uncle Hiram's hands. Remarkable! And that was your first experience with . . . praying for someone? You never did anything like that before?"

"No, ma'am."

"You didn't use anything like voodoo, or use a spell, or anything with magic?"

Ignorant! You never knew what some white people thought about Negroes. "Oh, no, ma'am! I prayed to God— the true God, like we do in church."

"I see. That's all right, then."

Would she get to the point? I hated standing before her, sweating in that hot, stuffy room. The old lady started to snore.

"Please excuse Miss Evelyn. She nods off all the time these days."

I waited: there was nothing else to do.

"Well, let me tell you what I need. My mind's so distracted these days, I can hardly think straight. Caleb, I want you to pray for my mother-in-law, ask God to restore her mind. She's lost, like a frightened child. When she's awake, she becomes agitated, cries, says hurtful things. My husband isn't home all day to deal with her, and I'm beside myself!"

I felt sorry for Miss Katie. But I still wished I was somewhere else. Praying for Uncle Hiram was one thing. But to pray for a white person? For Lee Davis's mama?

Miss Evelyn's mouth had gone slack. A dribble of spit ran down her chin, and Miss Katie wiped it away with a lacy white handkerchief. "You see how it is. It's ever so much worse when she's awake. Will you at least try?"

We both knew there was only one answer to her question. "Yes, ma'am. I be glad to. Anything to help y'all." I was a fool to agree and a liar to say I was happy about it. But Miss Katie was satisfied.

"Thank you! I've always liked your family, Caleb. Mr. Davis and I think so highly of Frank and Lucy, and of course we're so proud that Randall is serving our country."

Which is what *your* sorry son ought to be doing, I thought. But I said, "Thank you, Miz Katie. You want me to pray for Miz Evelyn now?"

"Yes, I do. But there's one thing I need to ask you first. Please don't mention to anyone that you've been here, especially not to Mr. Davis. He doesn't . . . uh, believe in this kind of thing. Knowing you were here would only upset him. You understand."

I stood before the old woman in the wheelchair. She was sound asleep, wheezing softly with each breath. Then it came to me: there might still be a way out. "When I prayed for Uncle Hiram, I put my hands on his."

Someone like me never, ever touched someone like Miss Evelyn. With luck Miss Katie would be mindful of that and send me on my way.

Her answer disappointed me. "Under the circumstances, it will be all right." She spread the white handkerchief on the old lady's shoulder. "There, now. Go ahead."

I couldn't wait to tell Nathan about this. He wouldn't believe me.

The woman's shoulder was all bones. I touched the handkerchief as lightly as I could. Get it over with, I ordered myself. Then you can get out of here.

"Go on," Miss Katie urged.

There was no going back. "Dear God, I asks you to reach down and heal Miz Evelyn. Lord, please give her back her right mind." My hand began to get warm, and I pulled it away.

"Something wrong?" Miss Katie asked.

"Uh, no, ma'am."

"Then what is it?"

"Nothing." No matter how I felt about it, this was no joke. It was time to get serious. I *had* to go on. I put my hand on the handkerchief again. "Pour down yo' healin' power into every part o' her. Clear her mind, so that Miss Evelyn ain't—"

She jolted awake so fast that I pulled my hand back again. She raised her head and peered at me with small, dark eyes. "Who are *you?*" she cried.

"Mother Davis, it's all right." Miss Katie tried to move between me and the woman in the wheelchair.

"What's this nigger doing in here?"

"Shhh, now. It's only Caleb. Caleb Brown. You know his daddy, Frank, and his mother, Lucy. Lucy used to do our laundry, remember?"

"Get this nigger boy away from me! I don't know

him. He doesn't belong here. Mama, come quick! Mama, I need you!"

"I'm sorry," Miss Katie told me. "This is how she is, so much of the time. She doesn't know what she's saying. Wait in the hall, and I'll get her calmed down."

I didn't need another invitation. Aunt Minnie met me coming out the door. "Go on in the kitchen," she whispered. "Wait there."

"Mama! Mama!" Miss Evelyn wailed. "I want to go home! Please, come take me home!"

I glanced behind me to see Aunt Minnie kneeling in front of her, murmuring soft words. Miss Katie was on the sofa, her hands over her face.

I headed for the kitchen, mad as hell. I had agreed to pray, and look what happened. The crazy old woman was pitiful, but saying those things to me . . .

I turned a corner and ran into Stewart Davis. Right away I smelled the liquor on him.

"What's goin' on? Hey, you're the dishwasher boy from the restaurant! What in Christ's name are *you* doin' here?"

"Your mama asked me here. She'll explain. I got to go now."

He moved to block my way. "I asked what you're doing in my house. And what's all that noise in the parlor?"

"Your grandma is upset. Your mama and Aunt Minnie are with her."

"What'd you do to her?"

"Nothing!"

He backed me against the wall. "You still ain't told me why you're in *my* house. Answer me!"

I was shaking.

And I was afraid.

"I ain't doin' nothing wrong. Miss Katie asked me to come."

"What for? She already got more of your kind working around here than we need."

The smell of booze on his breath was making me sick. He was so drunk that I knew I could take him, and for a second I thought about doing just that. "Please, Mr. Stewart. Just ask Miss Katie. She can explain."

"Don't try that on me. You got no good reason to be here. Now empty your pockets."

"Why? I don't got nothin' of yours."

"Your pockets!"

"No, sir! I ain't no thief, and your mama done invited me here." Now I wasn't afraid. I was spitting mad.

"A thief and a *liar* is what you are." Then he went for me. I dodged his fist, but he threw himself against me and we both went down. He grabbed at me, and I tried to twist away. And when he tried to choke me, I punched him right in the face.

I heard a door thrown open and the sound of someone running toward us. "What's going on here?" Miss Katie cried.

"I caught this nigger stealing from us!" Stewart shouted.

"Stop it! Both of you, stop it right now!"

I let go of him, and he fell on his back, panting.

"He was stealing, Mama!"

"I wasn't! I left the parlor like you asked me, Miss Katie, and Aunt Minnie told me to go to the kitchen and wait. Mr. Stewart run into me and wanted to know what I'm doin' here. I told him to ask you, but . . ."

Miss Katie looked at us sprawled on the floor, and sighed. "Run along, Caleb. I'm sorry."

"He's a thief! Make him empty his pockets."

"No, Stewart. I asked him here."

He pushed himself up and tried to stand but had to sit down again. "*Asked* him here? Why?"

"We'll discuss it later."

I got to my feet.

"Thank you for coming," Miss Katie told me. "I appreciate it. Please remember your promise."

"Yes, ma'am."

* * *

The long walk home gave me time to think things over. Agreeing to pray had been a mistake. That was certain. God hadn't asked me to do it: Miss Katie had. She was to blame for asking me in the first place. I *had* to do what she wanted. She was white.

At least she hadn't believed Stewart. I hated him so bad, it made my guts ache. Was I in trouble for what had happened? I remembered how it felt when my fist slammed into his face, and that made me glad. Then fear came over me so bad that I had to sit down under a tree.

I imagined all the things that could happen. Stewart would tell his daddy. Or he'd come looking for me with some of his friends. One morning, when I was walking to the Dixie Belle . . .

I made myself get up and head home. Everything's all right, I told myself. The bastard was so drunk, he won't even remember what happened. And Miss Katie doesn't want anyone to know why you were there. You only hit Stewart because you had to.

That wasn't quite true. I'd *wanted* to, and it felt great. I remembered that my hand had started to get warm as I prayed. What did that mean? And if things hadn't gone so wrong, what might God have been able to do?

CHAPTER NINETEEN

NOTHING MORE CAME of my fight with Stewart. I'd "gotten away with it"—at least that's how Nathan put it, and he said I was one lucky guy. Despite my promise, I'd told him the story. The Davises had treated me like dirt, and I wanted someone to take my side, soothe my hurt pride. Nathan did that, but of course he messed with me first, tried to scare me with talk about the Klan. I told him to shut up.

When Aunt Lou asked me why Miss Katie had wanted me at The Cedars, I lied and said it was to help move some heavy furniture so the maids could polish the floors.

Ma had told me that God would most likely speak to me again, but God did things in his own good time. Deep down I believed he wasn't finished with me, but in the meantime I couldn't relax.

Pop let the thing about God and me drop, never asked me about it. He stayed busy with his work—spent long days out and around, building and repairing things for folks, then often headed to his workshop after supper to do detail work that took his special tools. Ma said he did it to keep from worrying about Randall. She kept busy, too, but most everything she did was bound to make her think of Randall, like rolling bandages for the Red Cross and writing letters of sympathy to the families of Negro soldiers who'd gotten killed overseas, names she'd gotten from the Gold Star Mothers. She encouraged me to read the Bible, pray, and listen. But apart from that she was off in her own thoughts, as Pop was in his.

Nathan, Henry, and I took to going out almost every night, just to give ourselves something to do. But even that got old, with so few choices that weren't risky, illegal, or sinful—or all three. My days were cluttered with piles of dirty dishes and my nights with half-smoked cigarette butts. The summer dragged on; I was restless, bored, and ready for something to happen.

* * *

A couple weeks after my visit to The Cedars, Ma read out loud to Pop and me a short article under "Social News" in the *Davisville Herald*. "'We are happy to report that Mrs.

Evelyn Davis, who had been in poor health until recently, has enjoyed a dramatic recovery.'"

I sat up in my chair so fast that Pop looked at me. "You all right?" he asked.

"Yes, sir. I just needed to stretch."

Ma went on. "'Miss Evelyn, as her many friends call her, has gone to visit her daughter, Laura, and son-in-law, Lester, at their summer home on Tybee Island. When she returns to Davisville, Miss Evelyn will once again be living in her own place, rather than at The Cedars with her son Lee and his wife, Katie. We caught up with Miss Evelyn at a bridge party, and she told our reporter that she regards her complete recovery as nothing short of a miracle and "a new lease on life," and is grateful to Dr. Horace Gilliken for his excellent and attentive care.'" Ma put the paper down. "It's unheard of for someone as senile as she was to recover her mind. It does sound like a miracle."

"That ol' lady's brain *was* all to jelly, from what I hear," Pop said, uninterested.

I got up. "Caleb, what's wrong?" Ma asked. "You look strange."

"Nothing. It just feels hot in here. I'm going out for some air."

Even though God hadn't invited me to The Cedars and asked me to pray for the pitiful old lady who lived there, he'd answered my prayer. I knew I should feel glad for what

God had done for Miss Evelyn. Not long ago Ma had asked me to read that place in the Bible about his servant bringing the prisoners out of the prison. Now I was thinking of what that meant in a different way. If you didn't have your right mind, and if you had to sit in a wheelchair all the time, you were in a kind of prison. Maybe that's what it had been like for Miss Evelyn. And now—well, she was having a visit to Tybee Island. Somehow I'd helped her get free.

As I got undressed for bed, I thought about telling Ma. But I realized I wasn't going to. It was past time to start finding answers for myself.

I looked in the mirror above Randall's dresser. The face staring back at me was familiar, but it had some new short whiskers on its upper lip and chin. And the eyes were different somehow. They weren't the eyes of a kid anymore. I rolled up my sleeves and flexed my biceps, and they weren't the muscles of a kid, either. I realized I really was a man now. Still just a young man, like the folks had said on the day I got baptized, but not a boy anymore.

* * *

The telegram arrived two afternoons later. Ma wouldn't open it, so I ran to the shop to get Pop.

He fumbled with the thin envelope, but his big hands didn't want to work. At last he managed to get it open.

"Randall's dead," Ma whispered.

"No, he ain't. He ain't dead!"

"What, then?"

Pop's voice trembled. "'Regret to inform you PFC Randall Brown injured Monte Altuzzo, Italy. Taken prisoner, presumed en route to German POW camp. More information, contact Fifth Army and Red Cross. Sincere regrets, U.S. War Department.'" Pop crumpled the paper. "Taken prisoner."

"Frank! Oh, Lord, no!"

Pop pulled her into his arms.

"He's injured!" Ma cried. "A prisoner!"

"But he ain't dead," Pop declared. "He ain't dead!"

Ma reached out an arm, grabbed me, and held me close.

"He ain't dead," Pop said again. "He *ain't*. I know it."

Finally Ma let go of me. "What do we do, Frank?"

"We got to know just what's goin' on. I'm goin' to find Mr. Lee. He can take me to the camp. That Colonel Ross can help us."

"I'm coming with you," I said.

"Go hitch Sweetie while I get the word out. Lucy, you can't stay here all alone. You got to have some folks to keep you company till we back."

"Let Randall not be dead," I prayed over and over while I tied Sweetie to the wagon. "Please, God. I'll do anything you want. Anything. Just let him not be dead. Please, please let him be okay."

As I pulled the wagon around to the front of the house, Pop and Miss Suzy came hurrying into the yard. "You and Caleb run along now," she told Pop. "Lucy be in good hands till y'all get back."

Pop thanked her and told Sweetie to get going.

The drive to The Cedars seemed to take forever. Pop hardly said a word, but his face told it all. Anger and fear. My feelings mirrored his. Randall had been captured by the Germans. He was hurt—maybe so bad, he'd die. And if his injuries didn't kill him, he might be put to death in the prison camp. We might never see Randall again. We might never know what had happened to him. At that moment I hated the Germans with all my heart.

"Randall is gonna be okay," I told Pop, trying to sound like I believed myself.

"He ain't dead" is all Pop would say. "I feel it. He ain't dead."

At The Cedars, Lee Davis seemed genuinely upset when he heard our bad news. "Randall's a mighty good boy," he said. "Never caused any trouble. You and Lucy did a good job raisin' him, Frank. This shouldn't of happened. I'm sorry it did."

"Thank you, sir. I 'preciate that."

Pop didn't wait for Davis to ask what we needed. "Mr. Lee, telegram say for us to contact the army or the Red Cross for more information. You know Colonel Ross over at the camp. Would you please see if he might help us find out what happen to Randall?"

"Course I will, Frank. We can go right now. I'll have Byron get the car, and y'all can ride with me."

"Oh, no, sir. We can go in the wagon. But I do 'preciate it."

"All right. Y'all head on, and I'll meet you there."

At the camp Davis got us in to see Colonel Ross without delay. Ross was a thin white man behind a gray metal desk. He listened to Pop's story and read the crumpled telegram. He told us he was sorry, too, and promised to do everything he could to help us. "The fighting's been heavy along the Gothic Line," he said. "We've sustained many casualties, and a number of our boys have been captured."

"Telegram say they took him to a prison camp. Is that for sure?"

"Very likely. The Germans have some camps in Austria, and they would be closest to Italy. He might have been taken there, or maybe he's at Stalag Seven-A, in southern Germany. Lots of our boys end up there, too."

"How can we find out how bad he hurt?"

Ross looked serious. "Hard to tell. If your son made it to the camp alive . . ."

Pop's head dropped.

"I'm sorry, Mr. Brown."

I'd never heard a white man call my father "mister."

Ross went on. "If he made it to a camp alive, which he probably did, he might receive decent medical treatment. Food and supplies are probably scarce in the camps. But according to the Third Geneva Convention, every injured POW is entitled to medical treatment, food, and decent housing, just like we provide for our German prisoners here."

Pop must have forgotten he was talking to a white man. "But how can we find out if Randall is all right? Can he write to us? Can we write him, send him anything?"

"The Geneva Convention allows for prisoners to write and receive mail. The fellows here get letters and some packages from home—not so many now as they did at first, because things in Germany are going from bad to worse. The Red Cross can help sometimes. But once we know exactly where your son is being held, you should be able to write to him. With any luck he'll receive what you send and write back to you."

"Bill, I think a lot of Frank and his family," Davis told the colonel. "Randall's a fine boy. If there's anything you could do to help us, we'd sure appreciate it."

"I'll do whatever I can. The least we can do is help a local family when they need it. I'll make some calls and let you know what I find out."

"Thank you, sir," Pop said. "You and Mr. Lee is mighty kind to do this. We won't forget it."

"Don't mention it. As soon as I know something, I'll

send word out your way. In the meantime, we'll all say a prayer for your son's safety."

Pop was quiet as Sweetie walked us toward Toad Hop. "I hope that Ross can do somethin' more'n talk," he said at last. "If Randall ain't hurt too bad, he might have a chance."

"The Germans *have* to help him." I badly wanted to believe this. "Ross said so. It's what both sides agreed to."

"What it say on paper and what happen in the real world is two different things. And even if the Germans want to do what they suppose to, if they runnin' out of food and supplies, who you think they gonna look after first?"

"I hope Ross really can find out something."

"Me, too. Knowin' somethin'—*anythin'*, even if it bad news—is way better than not knowin'. Damn this war!"

Pop pulled Sweetie to a stop, dropped the reins, and put his hands over his face. His shoulders heaved, and a sound came out of him that I'd never heard before. It made me afraid—more afraid than I'd ever been. Pop couldn't fall apart. Suddenly I understood how much I counted on him to be his usual strong self.

"Hey, Pop, don't. It's going to be all right." I hesitated to touch him. Maybe he wouldn't want me to think he was weak and needed my comfort.

But he kept crying.

I put my arm around his strong shoulders. He didn't pull away.

After a minute Pop sat up straight again. He wiped his eyes and turned to me. "Sorry about that. My feelin's done took me by surprise. A man try to be strong for his family, but sometimes things get to be too much."

"I understand, Pop."

"What I wouldn't give to have your brother here with us now, all safe and sound. I sure am glad I got *you*."

Pop reached toward me, and we held each other right there, sitting side by side on the wagon seat, while Sweetie most likely wondered why we'd stopped in the middle of Brinson's Mill Road. For my part, I didn't care if everyone in the county saw us.

"I want this damn war over soon so *you* won't never have to go. I couldn't stand to have you gone, too."

"Randall's gonna make it. He'll come back. You'll see."

"Then you ask your God to keep him safe."

"Will you pray, too?"

"I might. You reckon the Lord'd listen to a old sinner like me?"

"I think so."

Pop patted my knee. "We'll see, then." He took the reins in his huge hands. "C'mon, Sweetie, let's get home. You know the way."

As we rode, I realized how completely my world had changed yet again in the short time since we'd gotten the telegram from the army. Just a couple days ago I'd been bored, ready for something to happen. And it had: Randall hurt, captured. It was my turn to want to cry.

* * *

We came home to a yard full of folks. Women were carrying food into the house, and the men who had been standing in the yard talking came and crowded around the wagon.

"Any news, Frank?"

"Randall really a prisoner?"

"You get any help from Davis?"

Pop told everyone what we knew. Inside we found Ma surrounded by the ladies of Toad Hop. Pots of food simmered on the stove, and the kitchen table was loaded with bowls and pans. Someone had brought a chocolate cake, and I realized I was hungry.

Ma pulled herself away from Miss Suzy and came to Pop and me. Pop told her Colonel Ross had promised to try to help.

Ma covered her eyes with her hands. "Please make everyone go home," she whispered. "They've all been so kind, but I have to be alone for a while."

"I understand, sugar. Folks," Pop called above the chatter of our company, "Lucy an' me shore 'preciate y'all comin' over to show us your concern. Randall ain't dead, though, just hurt. And from what the telegram say, taken prisoner. Colonel Ross over at the camp gonna do all he can to find out more, and soon as he do, we let y'all know, too. I thank you for all this food, and for your thoughtfulness. But right now we need to be alone. I know y'all understand."

Miss Suzy pushed herself up from the settee. "You heard the man! Let's give this family some peace."

The ladies filed out, all of them hugging Ma's neck and saying that if she needed anything at all, no matter what time of day or night, just let them know. They patted my shoulder and told Pop they'd be praying for us.

When everyone had gone, Ma looked around the kitchen and said she wondered where she was going to put all the food. She started putting things away, but she began to sob and couldn't stop. Pop led her to their room and closed the door behind them.

I found a plate and filled it with cold fried chicken, potato salad, slicing tomatoes, cornbread, and butter beans cooked with ham. How had people come up with all this food in the couple hours Pop and I had been gone? Part of me felt it wasn't right to want to eat just then, but I was starving and the food was right there.

When I cut myself a hunk of chocolate cake, I thought about the last time I'd eaten chocolate cake, when I'd shared it off the same plate with Andreas. With a German soldier. Someone like him had tried to kill my brother. Suddenly the cake didn't taste so good, and I put it down.

That night I looked in Randall's dresser and found his favorite shirt, a light blue work shirt worn soft from being washed so much. I put it on at bedtime and got into Randall's bed. Then I let myself think about him. How bad was he hurt? Or was he dead and we just didn't know it yet? If he was still alive, what camp was he in, and did he get help for his injuries?

Then I prayed—or tried to.

One thought wouldn't leave my mind: God had made Miss Evelyn well after I prayed for her. I hadn't really wanted to do that, and it caused me trouble afterward. Now God should do something for *me*. He had to make Randall be alive, make him recover from being hurt, and bring him home soon.

After all I'd done for God, it seemed to me that wasn't too much to ask.

* * *

I woke up sweating, my heart pounding. In my nightmare, Randall was dead and we were looking down at his body in the coffin. His army uniform was shredded and covered with blood, and his face was . . .

The sitting room clock said three thirty. I tried to sleep, but every time I closed my eyes, I saw Randall.

I went out the window and got Nathan up. He asked if we should get Henry, too, and I realized I wanted Henry along. He had the strong faith in God that I needed right now, and he'd say the right things, at least until Nathan shut him up.

Nathan asked if I wanted some of his daddy's moonshine. It didn't sound good to me, and Henry was still keeping the promise to "live clean" that he'd made on our baptism day, so Nathan didn't bother with the liquor. We headed to the pond.

On the dock, Nathan lit a cigarette. "It too bad about Randall," he began. "He gonna be okay, though, ain't he?"

"I already prayed for him," Henry said. "Bible say whatever we ask for in faith, God gonna do for us."

How much I wanted to believe that!

"War be over soon," Nathan went on. "Everybody say so. All Randall got to do is take it easy in that camp, the way the Germans do here, and soon he be comin' home."

I said nothing.

"Wonder how many Huns he killed. Sure to be some. If they was shootin' at *him,* he had to be shootin' back. Before you know it, he'll be sittin' on y'all's porch, drinkin' tea, braggin' about his medals."

His efforts to cheer me up weren't working. "Shut up, Nathan!" I cried.

"We only tryin' to help," Henry said.

"There's nothing to say."

"We know you hurtin'," Nathan said, "and we want to make you feel better. 'Sides, it ain't any fun just sittin' out here like three posts."

"Randall and me were here, right on this dock one night, just before he left."

"Oh? Y'all swim?" Henry asked.

"Yeah. And drank some bourbon he got at Tick's, and smoked. And . . . talked."

My friends were quiet, waiting.

"He told me that if anything happened to him, I should look after Pop and Ma. I told him nothing could happen." I was glad it was dark and they couldn't see me wipe my eyes on the sleeve of Randall's shirt.

"We sorry, Caleb," Henry said. "We right sorry for you and your folks. Want to swim? Take yo' mind off things?"

"Naw. We can just sit here."

So we did, for what seemed a long time. Then I jumped up. "Come on. Let's go to the creek."

We went through the dark woods and came to our usual spot by the big fishing log. I couldn't stay still, couldn't sit, couldn't relax and enjoy the cigarette Nathan offered me. I took two drags and threw it in the water.

"You nervous as a squirrel," Nathan said.

"Hit me."

"What you say?"

"Hit me. I want to fight."

"Hold on, now," Henry cried. "Caleb, what'sa matter with you?"

"I'll fight you both. Who wants to go first?"

"You crazy," Nathan told me. "We ain't got no reason to fight."

That's when I punched his shoulder. "Come on!" I cried. "Hit me!"

"You okay, man?"

My next punch landed on the side of his face. I hadn't planned to do it—didn't understand exactly why I was doing it.

"Son of a bitch, Caleb! What in hell's wrong with you?"

"Quit it!" Henry shouted.

I tackled Nathan, and we both went down. My fists went looking for his face, but he had his arms up now, and he began to fight back.

We rolled around in the moist sand by the creek, each trying to pin the other, trying to land punches. Henry kept out of our way, begging us to stop. Nathan broke free and jumped to his feet. "Come on!" he shouted. "Get up!"

"That's enough, now!" Henry shouted at me.

I was halfway up when Nathan landed his fist square on my chin. Then he was on top of me, going for my ribs, my side, my face. I was bigger and stronger, but he was madder, and determined to hurt me.

I got him in the face a couple times, then managed to push him off me and get back up. He leaped to his feet and stood facing me, panting, hands out in front, half to protect himself, half to find his next point of attack. "You ain't gonna quit *now,* is you?" he whispered.

Henry grabbed his arm. "Stop, Nathan! Caleb, quit, now! Ain't you two had enough?"

Nathan shoved him aside. "Try and finish what you begun," he taunted, "if you ain't a coward as well as a bully."

I lunged for him, and his knee caught me right in my crotch. As I went down, moaning, I remembered Nathan was good at that move—Dolan Hill would never forget it. I lay on the sand, gasping, holding myself, wishing I could get up and kill Nathan. But I couldn't.

He looked down at me. "Had enough? I got more where that come from."

"I give. Nathan, you fight dirty, you know that?"

"What's *wrong* with you, Caleb? You gone crazy or something? I didn't do nothin' to you."

"Help me up."

"Not until you promise that this is over."

"I promise." Nathan pulled me to my feet. The ache in my groin wouldn't quit, and they half carried me to the fishing log.

Nathan kept his distance. He pulled out his cigarettes and offered me one. I took it, and this time it tasted good. Then he shoved the pack in Henry's direction, and to my surprise he took one, too.

We smoked the cigarettes all the way down before anyone said anything.

"You all right now?" Nathan asked.

"Fightin' ain't no way to solve nothin'," Henry put in.

"Tell that to General Eisenhower," I said.

"Seriously, Caleb. You okay?" Nathan asked.

I nodded. "Yeah."

"What got into you?"

"I dunno. I just had to hit something."

"Gee, thanks! So now I'm a 'something.'"

"Don't take it like that."

"All right, but I'm doin' you a big favor not to be mad as hell. You really all right?"

"Except for these," I said, putting my hand on my crotch. "Why'd you have to do that?"

"'Cause it works, brother. And you was goin' crazy."

"Guess I just got mad—you know, Randall and all."

"And they ain't nobody to get back at, right?" Henry asked.

"Right."

"'Cept your best friend," Nathan said quietly.

I didn't want Henry to get his feelings hurt. "*One* of my best friends. Sorry."

"Forget it. I understand."

"We better get home."

At his window Henry whispered he'd be praying for us. Knowing that made me feel better.

Nathan put his hand on my shoulder when we got to his place. "You let me know what I can do," he said gruffly.

"Just don't ask me to fight you again, 'cause that'd be one invitation I'd have to decline."

He was still trying to cheer me up. That made me feel better, too.

At home I turned on the light in my room and checked myself in the mirror. My chin ached, and there would be a bruise, and there was a cut across my right cheekbone. Dried blood was smeared all down my face. My clothes were wrecked—Nathan had torn Randall's shirt, and his blood was on the front. Both the shirt and my pants were filthy from rolling on the ground.

I'd have to tell the folks, try to explain.

The clock in the front room chimed five times. In an hour I'd have to get up to go to work. I took off Randall's shirt, ruined now, and dropped it on the floor.

CHAPTER TWENTY

I OVERSLEPT. Ma had to wake me. She touched the tangled clothes with her foot. "Caleb? What have you been doing?"

Pop appeared behind her. Maybe I was covered with bruises and cuts, more than I noticed last night. I pulled the covers up to my neck.

"What the hell?" Pop demanded. "You been fightin' again?"

"I can explain, Pop."

"Yeah, I bet! Ain't we got enough trouble in this house without you addin' to it?"

"It's not what you think."

"How you know what I think? Let's talk about what I can *see*. And ain't this your brother's shirt?"

Ma picked it up and held it to her face.

"Sugar, please go start the coffee. Caleb and me'll be along shortly."

Ma murmured something about washing and mending it and left.

Pop glared down at me. "Get up," he ordered.

"I'm not dressed."

"Get up!"

I threw back the covers and started to get to my feet, then had to sit down. I ached all over and felt a sharp pain in my right side. As bad as my body hurt, my heart hurt worse. Just yesterday Pop and I had made up with each other, but now I'd wrecked it all. Here we were, back to the old war between us.

Pop rooted in my dresser. "Here," he said, tossing me a pair of drawers. I pulled them on, then sat back down on the bed.

"Let's go outside."

Instantly I was on my guard. "Why? I won't let you whip me, Pop, no matter what." The fingers on my right hand were twitching.

"Who said anything about a whippin'? You covered with mud. And ain't you looked at your face? That cut might need a doctor."

In the yard Pop filled the water bucket and gave me a cloth to wash myself.

"Now talk," he said when I was done. "First of all, where was you last night, and who you been fightin' with?"

I told him everything. For the first time I could ever remember, I was completely honest, and I didn't feel the need to defend myself. I explained about my nightmares, about waking up and being afraid to go back to sleep, about climbing out my window and getting Nathan and Henry. About us talking at the pond, and then about wanting— about *needing*—to fight somebody at the creek.

Pop lit up his pipe and smoked. I kept waiting for him to get mad, maybe even order me to the shop, but he just looked thoughtful. Sad, even. When I was finished, he didn't say anything.

"Why did I want to fight Nathan, Pop? It just came over me, and I couldn't help it. He didn't do anything to me."

He didn't answer right away. Then he said, "Same reason I reckon a man get home from losin' his job and kick his favorite dog that come runnin' out to meet him."

"I don't understand."

"Think about it, son. Who you really mad at? It ain't Nathan or Henry. What's got you so riled up?"

Although the morning was already warm, I suddenly felt cold, standing in the yard wearing only my drawers.

I looked at the ground. "Lots of things. The war, the news about Randall. The way I've been treated at the Dixie Belle—"

"You didn't say nothin' to me 'bout that."

Now I looked at my father, hoping he'd understand.

"Sound like you and me got a lot to talk about," Pop said.

At that moment I was ready to tell him everything else: about Voncille, my friendship with Andreas, going to The Cedars and fighting with Stewart Davis...

"Coffee's ready," Ma called from the kitchen door.

"C'mon," Pop said. "We can talk about this later. After breakfast, if you want." He put his arm around my shoulders as we went toward the door.

"I'm late for work already."

"The Dixie Belle can get along without you for a couple hours. Lou'll tell 'em you need the morning off, after all we been through since yesterday."

Over breakfast I told my story to Ma. "When we got to the creek, I felt all ... stirred up. Like there was a swarm of hornets trapped inside me, fighting to escape. I never planned to punch Nathan. It just happened."

"I know why he done it," Pop said. "He just needed a way to get all his feelin's out. You understand, Lucy."

Ma glared at him. "Of *course* you know why he did it, Frank! You've always done the same thing, and that's how you've raised him. Randall, too. But I *don't* understand. I never did, and now I don't think I want to." Her words came out in a flood. "Why must you men always turn to *fighting* as the way to 'get your feelings out'? Why must violence always be the answer to every problem? You whipped your sons for years because you figured that was the only way to get them to obey you. It didn't work! Do you know that Randall and Caleb went behind your back to do things you never would have allowed? Like climbing out their window night after night, month after month, to go and do God knows what—"

"Ma, don't!" Panic was rising in me. I wanted to jump up, get out of that room, run far away where no one would ever find me. Pop pressed my shoulder so I couldn't move.

Ma kept her eyes fixed on him. "Do you know how long your sons have been smoking and drinking? Or when Randall first started going to Rose's place?"

"Ma, how do you know—?"

Now she looked at me. "Oh, Caleb, I have eyes! And a nose, too. You think I can't smell cigarettes on your clothes? You think I never smelled the perfume on Randall's shirts or saw the lipstick stains on them? You think I never smelled liquor on him in the mornings, or on you? You were out getting drunk the night before your baptism, weren't you?"

I was too dumbfounded to say a word. Pop was silent, too.

"You look surprised," Ma went on. "And maybe you're wondering why I never said anything to your father."

"Yes, ma'am. I do wonder that."

Ma looked back at Pop. "Because I knew that if I did, there'd be even more whippings in this house, and I couldn't stand that! Caleb, you and your friends just had to fight the Hill brothers, didn't you? And last night you had to get into it with your best friend. And why? 'To get your feelings out'! Both times, someone could have been hurt badly. What if the Hill boys had had a knife? What if you'd choked your friend to death?"

"I would never do that!"

"That's easy to say now, but you don't know, just like you'll never know what could have happened all those nights you and your brother and your friends went out looking for trouble. First it's fists—what'll it be next time? Guns? Bombs? More wars?"

Ma was shouting and crying all at once. "What's *wrong* with you—with *all* you men?"

She stood up and wiped the tears off her face. "I'm going to wash Randall's shirt and hang it out to dry. Then I'm going to mend and iron it. *Women's* work. It doesn't hurt anyone! It tries to fix things, makes things decent. Caleb, you're not to touch that shirt again. Your brother will want to wear it when he comes home." Ma grabbed the metal bucket where Randall's shirt was soaking and hurried out the back door.

I got up to go after her, but Pop held me back. "Let her be for now."

Pop and I looked at each other. I kept waiting for him to explode, but he just looked old and tired.

"I'm going to work," I said.

"All right. Take your mind off things for a while."

"Thanks for understanding, Pop. About my fight."

"You still buddies with Nathan?"

"Yeah. About all the other stuff—"

"We can talk about that later on. I got to go be with your ma right now."

"I never saw her so upset."

"Me either. Wish I knew what I was gonna say to her."

"I didn't mean to cause trouble."

"It's a lot more than you scrappin' with Nathan. Don't worry. Your ma's gonna be all right. Go on to work. If I find out anything more about your brother, I'll come by the Dixie Belle."

That was the first time Pop had ever mentioned coming by the café. But anything seemed possible now.

* * *

When I got to the alley behind the Dixie Belle, there was Andreas, emptying a garbage pail. My stomach knotted.

"Caleb?" he asked. *"Wie geht's?"*

I knew he was asking how I was. But I couldn't answer. I didn't want to see him. He was one of *them*—and they had hurt my brother, maybe killed him. My hands clenched.

But Andreas was my friend, too. "I got to let them know I'm here," I muttered, pushing by him.

"Caleb?" he called after me. I kept going.

In the kitchen Aunt Lou asked how I was and how Ma and Pop were taking the news. She said Ma shouldn't have to bear such a burden—no woman should. How I needed to be strong for both my parents. And how she'd been praying for Randall ever since she'd heard the bad news, and that God would protect him.

I let her go on. Uncle Hiram just put his hand on my shoulder and told me how sorry he was and that everyone in Toad Hop was praying for Randall, and for all of us.

Betty Jean told me she was sorry. Even Miss Sondra said the same.

Aunt Lou kept Andreas busy doing chores away from the sink. I caught him looking at me once, and I guessed he wanted to talk, but I wouldn't give him an opening. Maybe later, maybe after I had the chance to get ahold of myself. At the moment, I just wished he weren't there, would disappear back to Germany. Wished I'd never met him.

The dinner hour wasn't busy, so Aunt Lou told me I could have a break. I was glad for a chance to get away for a while, try to sort things out. Aunt Lou made me an iced tea and told me to take my time.

I went into the alley and walked away from the garbage cans. A pecan tree shaded the narrow lane between the back of the Dixie Belle and the tall wooden fences on the other side. The day was hot, so I went under the tree to get out of the sun.

Right away, here came Andreas. I wasn't ready to talk to him, but sooner or later we'd have to speak, so it might as well be now.

He got right down to it. "I hear about your brother—"

"Randall."

"*Ja. Ich weiss.* He is hurt?"

"Yeah."

"Bad hurt?"

I shrugged. "We don't know."

"*Und er ist jetzt ein Kriegsgefangener.*"

"What? Speak English."

He shook his head. "I will try. *Dein Bruder,* your brother, is a prison—"

"A prisoner. Yeah. A prisoner of war. Just like you."

"*Du bist sauer auf mich?*" He was eyeing me carefully.

"I said to speak English!"

"I am sorry," Andreas said. "It is hard for me—when—*ich bin,* how do you say . . . ?"

"How do I say *what?*" I was ready for this guessing game to end. "Give me a cigarette."

He pulled the pack out of his shirt pocket and lit a cigarette for me when I had it in my mouth. After a couple of drags, I felt calmer.

"You are, uh, mad with me?" Andreas asked. "Because of Randall?"

I didn't want to tell him the truth. "I don't know. *Ich weiss nicht.*"

He smiled. "You learn some German, *ja?*"

"*Ja.*"

"*Ich glaube*—I think you are mad with me, and so I cannot, uh, talk so good. And my English—she flies away then, *wie ein Vogel.*" He made a flying gesture with his hands. "Randall is hurt, I am sorry. It is a bad thing. I think of *meinen Bruder,* Reinhardt, and how he is dead."

I'd forgotten that. My brother was injured but might be alive. Reinhardt was dead. Ma and Pop and I still had hope; Andreas's family—none.

"I'm sorry, Andreas. About Reinhardt."

Aunt Lou appeared in the alley. "Hate to break in, but Sondra is wonderin' where y'all are. I tried to tell her you could use some time, but business come first with that fine lady."

We followed her back into the kitchen. The dirty dishes had piled up beside the sink, where just a few minutes ago there had been none.

I started to scrape plates into the metal pail beside the sink. Andreas touched my shoulder. "Stop . . . a minute."

I let the messy plate slide into the hot, soapy water. "What?"

"May I . . . ?"

He opened his arms toward me, palms up. Maybe Andreas didn't know the English word, but his meaning was clear.

"Okay."

Then he stepped toward me and put his arms around me. I put mine around him, and the tears came.

I heard the squeaky swinging door to the dining room being pushed open. Then the sound of steps.

"Well, if that ain't a sickening sight," Voncille declared.

Andreas and I let go of each other. I felt embarrassed.

"Voncille, this ain't none o' your business," Aunt Lou said. "Just don't you say another word."

"Shut up, old lady! I'll say what I want." Voncille advanced on me. "I promised myself I'd never waste another word on *you,* but as a patriotic, self-respecting American, I can't keep quiet."

Instantly I was fighting mad. "Say it, then."

"With pleasure. What in the name of God is wrong with you, boy? The Krauts blow your brother all to pieces, take him prisoner, and you're in here *lovin'* on one of 'em? Ain't you got an ounce of pride? Or maybe you'd like this pretty boy here to do more to you than just hug your neck."

"You hush your dirty mouth!" Aunt Lou shouted. "You make me sick, talkin' like that!"

"Lou's right," Uncle Hiram put in. "We all done had enough o' yo' white-trash mouth."

Then Sondra Davis elbowed her way through the swinging door. "You all at it again?" she asked. "I swear to God, I'm ready to fire every last one of you and find some decent help."

"You don't have to fire *me,*" I said. "I'm done." Since my first day, that woman—and Voncille, too—had been pushing me toward some invisible line. They'd wanted to force me to cross it, find some excuse to fire me. But I had stepped over the line on my own, and I felt like I'd just won a race at the Olympics. I was more than ready to get away from the Dixie Belle and go home.

"I quit, too," Aunt Lou announced.

"Count me in," Uncle Hiram added.

I didn't wait to see what would happen next. "See you around," I told Andreas. "You're the only white person who ever tried to be my friend." He probably didn't understand what I said, but that was okay.

But Voncille understood. "How nice for you both," she sneered as I headed for the back door.

"Caleb!" Andreas called after me.

I didn't turn back. I had to get home to my father. When I got there and told him everything, he would put his strong arms around me and say it was all going to be okay.

* * *

But the next week was terrible. Pop was right—not knowing about Randall was much worse than getting bad news. I helped the folks all I could, and the ladies kept bringing food. Each evening Ma lit a candle in the window where her Blue Star Mother banner was hanging.

Then at last we heard. A soldier from the camp drove out in a jeep and delivered the message: Randall was alive. He'd been captured and taken by the Germans to the camp called Stalag 17-B near Krems, Austria. A mortar shell had blown off his left hand and blinded his left eye, but he was not in danger of dying from those injuries. That was all Colonel Ross had been able to find out.

Ma took it real hard. She'd made herself keep going until now, but the strain made her sick. She went to bed and stayed there, with the curtains closed, for two days.

All that time I kept seeing Randall with half his face gone. He'd been blinded in one eye—did that mean the whole eye had been blown out of its socket? Was it just an empty hole oozing yellow pus? Was his skin all burned off, and did he look like Frankenstein's monster? When he came home, would I be able to look at him and not feel sick?

And what about losing his hand? That was even worse than losing his eye. All Randall's dreams for after the war were dead now. So many jobs were impossible if you had to try to do them with one hand. He'd have to come back and live in Toad Hop with us, but he'd hate it. Maybe right this minute he was wishing he'd been killed. The second I thought that, I tried to erase it from my mind.

When I went into Pop's shop the second day, I found him sitting at the workbench, staring at his left hand.

He didn't bother to look up. "What that brother o' yours gon' do now? Nobody ever heard of a one-handed carpenter! All his plans—goin' to Atlanta, workin' up there in his friend's business . . ."

"You would have let him go?"

Pop sighed. "Course I would. Even back then, when he was home and fightin' with me about his future, I knew I couldn't stop him. Now I realize I should of encouraged him. Randall was right. There ain't no future 'round here. You got to get out, too, Caleb, when you can."

"I'll stay here and work with you, Pop. Help take care of Randall, if he needs me."

"It ain't fair!" he cried. "A workin' man need his hands—*both* hands!"

"We'll help him," I said, trying to find some way to make things better. "Randall is tough. He won't let this stop him."

Pop looked at me. "He better be tough, son. Tough enough to make it in that camp without a doctor, or even food, for all we know. Tough enough to keep livin' so he can come home—and then fight a war all over again, against *this* goddamn place! The Nazis that run Davisville won't give an *able-bodied* Negro a fair chance, let alone a black man with only . . ."

He couldn't finish.

You healed Uncle Hiram, I told God silently. And Miss Evelyn. Why didn't you . . .

I was afraid to finish my question, but it was there even if I didn't give it words: Why didn't you answer my prayers and keep Randall from getting hurt at all? I tried to tell myself that if I hadn't prayed, Randall might have been killed. Getting hurt and captured was bad, but it was better than getting killed. Maybe I hadn't prayed hard enough, or often enough, or correctly enough. That's why I hadn't gotten everything I wanted. But that made prayer into some kind of contest between me and God, one I could never win.

Later I had another thought. When Randall came home, if he asked me, would I have the guts to pray for him, ask God to grow him a new hand? A new eye? Brother

Johnson loved to preach on the text that said "With God, all things are possible." Could that include an injured man getting new body parts? That *did* sound like something right out of *Frankenstein*.

I prayed, Please bring Randall home. If you do—I mean, *when* you do—I'll pray for him. I'll do anything. Just let him come home.

CHAPTER TWENTY-ONE

WHEN I GOT UP the third morning, I found Ma cooking breakfast. She apologized for going all to pieces and asked if I wanted my eggs scrambled or fried over easy. Then, while I was eating, Pop came in and said we needed to do something to take our minds off our worries. He proposed we go into Davisville together, do some shopping, mail the letters we'd all written to Randall care of the Red Cross, and have dinner at Uncle Billy's Barbecue. Ma agreed. I asked if Nathan and Henry could go along, and Pop said it would be okay.

In town my friends and I drifted and bought ourselves Coca-Colas. Soon it was getting on toward noon, and we had to meet the folks. Uncle Billy's was a couple blocks from Main Street, and as we headed there, we found ourselves at the Dixie Belle.

I hadn't been by the restaurant since the day I quit. It looked the same. There was the big window where we'd stood the day it opened. The place was pretty full, but the booth on the other side of the glass was empty. Nothing looked as shiny and new as it had that first day.

I wondered about the new cooks. The food couldn't be near as good as when Aunt Lou and Uncle Hiram were there. And what about Andreas? Was he still washing dishes? Maybe he'd been beaten up in the camp again. That made me think of Randall and wonder how he was being treated.

"We gotta go," Nathan said. "My stomach says so."

"Mine, too," Henry agreed. "Come on."

But then something inside the Dixie Belle caught my eye. I looked, and looked again to make sure. "Hey. In there."

They put their faces up to the glass. The glare made it hard to see inside, so I put my hands on either side of my face to block the sunlight. "Am I seeing right?"

"I see white folks eatin' dinner," Nathan answered. "That ain't news."

"Yeah, but look all the way to the back."

He did. "Oh." Then, "Well, what you expect?"

"What?" Henry asked.

"All the way back, dummy. Along the wall. At the long table," Nathan told him.

I couldn't stop staring. At the back of the dining room, crowded around a couple of tables, were German prisoners, enjoying their dinners. Among them sat Andreas, talking and laughing just like all the rest.

I felt like someone had punched me in the gut.

"What'sa matter?" Nathan asked. "Davis can feed anybody he wants."

"One of those guys is Andreas."

Nathan's eyes got wide. "Your buddy? The one that got you fired for huggin' him?"

"That wasn't the reason! And I didn't get fired. I quit, remember?"

"Okay. So why you all upset now? You don't even work here anymore. Good riddance, I say."

How could I make Nathan and Henry understand? Somewhere thousands of miles away, Randall was in a prison camp, one hand blown off and one eye gone. If he was still alive, he sure as hell wasn't eating a fried chicken dinner in a German restaurant with the local folks.

I looked at Andreas again. Seeing him there made me want to crash through the window and get my hands around his neck. I felt betrayed.

"Let's go," Nathan said. "Let the crackers enjoy themselves."

"You said it," Henry added. "Come on, Caleb."

They were right. There was nothing I could do. Lee Davis owned the Dixie Belle, and he was free to serve anyone he wanted—and refuse service, too. That didn't help my feelings, though. I recognized those feelings: the same ones that made me throw a punch at Nathan the other night. That made me piss all over the crates of collards and potatoes. That made me slash Stewart Davis's tires. Ma's words rang in my head: "What's wrong with you? With *all* you men?"

I pulled myself away from the window and followed Nathan and Henry around the corner. I had to stop, though, because I was shaking so bad.

The door to the restaurant was right ahead of us. A young couple went in, then two pretty white girls. They noticed us, and I realized we were standing so close to the door that we were halfway blocking it.

"Caleb, you all right?" Henry asked. "You look sick."

"I'm fine. Come on."

We started down the sidewalk, but I stopped again. It wasn't right. It wasn't fair. But there was nothing I could do about it. Besides, my folks were waiting. Best just forget it.

No. Not this time. Not ever again, no matter what might happen. What should I do? I prayed silently.

God didn't answer, and suddenly I understood that I already knew what to do. All I needed now was the courage to do it.

I turned around and headed back to the Dixie Belle.

"Hey, Caleb! What are you doin'?" Nathan scurried after me, Henry right behind him.

I got to the door of the café. "What is it?" Nathan asked.

"I'm going in there and ask to be served. You guys can come with me if you want."

Nathan looked at me like I'd just grown horns. "Don't be crazy, man! You can't go in there. They'll—"

"They'll do what?"

"I dunno. Throw you out. Hurt you. Come on, Caleb. Your folks are waitin'."

"If you won't come with me, you and Henry go to Uncle Billy's and tell them I'll be there after a while, but not to order me any food. I'm eating in the Dixie Belle."

Henry yanked on my sleeve. "No, you ain't! Just forget it. You go in there, it gonna be trouble—worse trouble than anything you ever been in before."

"I don't care. I've had enough. Haven't you?"

"Sure I have," Nathan said. "You're right. Course you are. But this ain't the way to do things. You *know* that. We gotta be patient. Wait for the right time. And this ain't it."

"You're wrong. This *is* the right time. Remember why we threw those rocks at the prisoners and fought the Hill boys? You said you were sick of being treated like dirt. I am, too. Here's our chance to fight back—in a different way."

"I want to, man! Really, I do. But—"

"It ain't too late!" Henry pleaded. "You don't got to do this!"

I understood the fear in their eyes, because it was in me, too. "It's okay," I told them. "I understand. Next time, all right?"

Nathan nodded. "Be careful."

"I'll see you at Uncle Billy's."

He squeezed my shoulder and hurried away, pulling Henry behind him.

Alone, I pushed the door open and made myself walk through it. My heart was jumping around inside my chest.

The room was noisy, full of happy voices, clattering dishes, and music on the jukebox. The prisoners at the big table seemed to be having a fine time, judging from their laughter. Delicious, familiar smells came from the kitchen.

Right in front of me was an empty table. I sat down and waited. Then I felt eyes on me, and people at the next table got quiet. I studied the menu and waited some more.

Betty Jean appeared. "Caleb, what are you doin'? Get out of here."

"I'd like a fried chicken dinner with collards, yams, cornbread, and a cup of coffee."

"You can't eat in here!" she whispered fiercely. "Go on, 'fore there's trouble."

"A chicken dinner, please."

"Caleb!"

Here came Voncille. "What in the hell are you doin'?" she demanded. "You got some nerve comin' around here. Now git! You know we don't serve colored. You want yourself somethin' to eat, go on over to Uncle Billy's."

"I don't want barbecue. I'm going to eat here."

"We don't serve *niggers*."

The word jangled in my head, and I had to steady myself. "I don't want any trouble. I'm hungry, and I have money. Please bring me a chicken dinner."

Lee Davis burst through the kitchen door.

"Mr. Lee, I tried to tell him, but—"

"It's all right, Voncille. You run along and take care o' your customers. I'll handle this."

I glanced around. Everyone in the room, including the German prisoners, was staring in our direction.

"Folks, y'all go back to your meals. We got ourselves a little misunderstanding here. This boy'll be gone in just a minute."

People started talking again. I knew they were talking about me.

"Caleb, what are you doin' in here?" Lee Davis began, kind of friendly. "I'm surprised. You know we got good places in town for colored folks to enjoy a meal with their own kind. We got nice places for white folks, too, and the Dixie Belle is one of 'em. Your people and mine don't eat together—everybody knows that. So you just run along and I'll forget all about this."

"My brother went off to the war," I said, slow and loud. Folks started to get quiet again. "He was wounded fighting against the Germans. They blew off his hand and blinded one eye. And now he's in one of their prisons—a bad one. He might die there!" I was practically shouting.

A woman at the next table put down her iced tea.

"We don't know what's happening to Randall, but I bet he's not in a restaurant eating with Germans!"

I heard people muttering.

"But if *they're* good enough to eat here"—I pointed to where the prisoners sat—"so am I."

Davis looked at me with cold, hard eyes, but he kept his voice calm. "It's like I said before: whites and colored don't socialize in this town, and that includes the Dixie Belle. What say you and me go outside, talk things over, and let these good people finish their dinners?"

"I'm not leaving until I get a meal."

"That's enough!" Davis growled. "Get him outta here."

Two big white men appeared behind Davis. One of them yanked me to my feet and started pushing me to the door. I looked across the room and saw Andreas staring at me. "You said you were my friend!" I shouted at him. "Do something!"

He tried to stand up, but the man next to him pushed him down.

I was dragged through the door and shoved to my knees. Davis appeared and looked down at me. Other folks stopped to watch.

"Stand up." Davis told me. I got to my feet. His men held my arms.

"Can you behave now?" Davis asked. "You better, unless you want real trouble. My men ain't gonna let go until you promise."

"I haven't done anything wrong. Randall could be dying in a Nazi camp, and you let *them* eat in there! Why?"

He just looked at me. "You all done?"

I pushed my fear back and kept going. "So if Randall showed up in his uniform and wanted dinner, you wouldn't serve him, either."

"That's right. Colored got their own places to eat in my town."

Stewart appeared beside his father.

"How come you're not off fighting?" I asked him. "All the *real* men are."

"Good question," a bystander said.

"It's because you're yellow," I told Stewart.

He came roaring at me. I tried to go for him, ready to

settle things once and for all, but one of Davis's men held me back, and the other grabbed Stewart.

"Let me go! I'll kill him!" Stewart cried.

"Get back inside," Davis ordered. "Tell Voncille to cut me a piece o' lemon pie. I'll be right there."

"Just you wait, nigger!" Stewart shouted. "This ain't over by a long shot."

"I'll be ready."

"Both y'all, shut up!" Davis commanded. "Didn't I tell you to get back inside?" Stewart obeyed.

"Show's over," Davis told the curious crowd. "There ain't gonna be a fight. Go on, now."

Folks moved away, and that left Davis, his men, and me.

"Let him go," Davis told the guy holding me. He took a deep breath and closed his eyes for a moment, like he was trying to be patient. "Caleb, you might not believe this, but I'm your friend."

"Yeah?"

"Yeah. I've always been a friend to the Brown family, and to all the folks out in Toad Hop. I didn't have to get electricity out your way, but I did, 'cause I like y'all. I think a lot of Frank and Lucy—Randall, too. When I heard the news about him, I felt real bad. That's why I did all I could with Colonel Ross. You think he'd of gone to all that trouble for y'all if I hadn't asked him? Y'all are like family, and I'll do whatever I can to help you, Randall, and your folks—anybody out in Toad Hop. But you know the rules, and you got to abide by 'em. Go against the rules, and I won't lift a finger for you."

I kept my eyes fixed on the sidewalk, where a black ant was dragging a scrap of food toward the street.

Davis addressed his men. "You boys go on and have you some coffee and pie. Caleb and me are all right now."

"You sure, boss?"

Davis looked at me. "Yeah. Everything's fine."

Now it was just Davis and me.

"You've been playing a game with me for a good long time, haven't you?"

I didn't know what he meant. "Sir?"

"'Sir.' I like that. That's better. But you don't really want to call me sir, do you, now?"

I kept my eyes down.

"Look at me, goddamn it!"

I did.

"That shuffling and that nigger talk you use around me—that's all an act. Like the day you came begging for a job. Somebody taught you the game real good, but they never got the most important lesson down into your *soul*. That's why you think you're just as good as a white man. That's right, ain't it?"

I wouldn't look away.

"Answer me!"

"Yes, sir. I do."

Davis's face was bright red, and his forehead was wet with sweat. He took a step toward me. "You—"

"Caleb? Mr. Lee? What in the name of—"

Pop was running across Main Street toward us. I saw Ma, Nathan, and Henry on the far sidewalk.

"Mr. Lee, what's wrong?" Pop asked.

Davis wiped his face. "Caleb and me was just having a little talk. He came into my restaurant and acted like he could eat there, so I had to remind him of a couple things. That's all."

Ma and the others came up behind Pop.

"I swear, Mr. Lee, Caleb ain't been hisself," Pop said. "He don't know what he's doin'."

"I do, too!"

"Caleb!" Pop cried. "You best apologize right now."

I turned to the others. "There are German prisoners in there eating, Ma! Andreas is in there!"

"Hush," Ma pleaded.

"No, Ma. And Randall's—"

Pop cut me off. "We all been so upset over Randall," he told Lee Davis.

"Yeah, we know," Davis replied. "He's been hurt, and captured, and we're all right sorry. I feel bad for y'all, I truly do. And I pray Randall makes it home when the war is over. Who knows? Maybe he's a war hero, gonna come home with a Bronze Star or something. But that wouldn't change things around *here*. It don't mean we can't all be friendly, work together, help each other out. But in Davisville, Georgia, the races ain't ever gonna mix, 'specially not in my restaurant."

"We understand," Pop said. "But you know how this younger generation is. They got all these ideas in they heads—"

"Pop, quit making excuses! You know I'm right. And you're wrong," I told Davis.

"I'll let that pass . . . this one time," he replied. "Take your boy home, Frank. I never had a n— a colored boy talk to me the way he just did. Can't say I like it. But I'm gonna let it pass. Now you best get him home. I'm tired of his face." Davis went back into the Dixie Belle.

"Come on," Pop said, "before that son of a bitch change his mind." He put his hand on my shoulder. "You're a fool to go up against Lee Davis. But you got more guts than I do, and that's the truth."

My heart was bursting, but not with fear. "I had to do it. For Randall."

"For all of us," Ma said softly.

Pop looked inside the Dixie Belle and sighed. "I pray one day folks like us'll be able to go in a place like that and enjoy a decent meal. Sure do smell good, don't it?" He closed his eyes for a moment. "You know, it's past our dinnertime. Hope Uncle Billy still got plenty o' barbecue and ribs, 'cause I could eat a horse. How 'bout y'all?"

"I'm *way* past ready," Nathan declared.

"Me, too!" Henry added.

All of a sudden, I was starving. "Let's go," I said.

"We're proud of you, son," Pop said quietly. He gazed down the empty sidewalk. "Let's go get us some dinner. It's all over now."

I reached out to my parents and my two best friends, and then they had their arms around me. "No, Pop," I told him. "It's not all over. It's just beginning."